Jalapeño Cheddar Cornbread Murder

Jalapeño Cheddar Cornbread Murder

Jodi Rath

Published by MYS ED llc
PO Box 349
Carroll, OH 43112

First Printing, June 21, 2019

Leavensport, Ohio

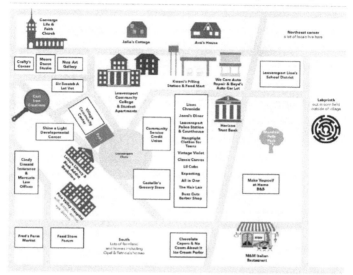

Converge Life & Faith Church

Julie's Cottage

Ava's House

Northeast corner
a lot of locals live here

Crafty's Corner

Moore Dance Studio

Nuu Art Gallery

Sir Scratch A Lot Vet

Leavensport Community College & Student Apartments

Kwani's Filling Station & Food Mart

We Care Auto Repair & Bayel's Auto Car Lot

Leavensport Lion's School District

Cast Iron Creations

Village Community Center

Pool

Shine a Light Developmental Center

Community Service Credit Union

Lions Chronicle

Jenni's Diner

Leavensport Police Station & Courthouse

Hangtight Clothes for Teens

Horizon Trust Bank

Labyrinth
out in corn field
outside of village

Cindy Cincaid Insurance & Mercurio Law Offices

Leavensport Library & Rock Mobile Bookmobile

Leavensport Chats

Vintage Violet

Classic Curves

Lil Cubs

Castello's Grocery Store

Expecting

All in One

The Hair Lair

Buzz Cuts Barber Shop

Mountain Falls Park

Make Yourself at Home B&B

Fred's Farm Market

Feed Store Forum

South
Lots of farmland
and homes including
Opal & Patricia's homes

Chocolate Capers & No Cones About It Ice Cream Parlor

M&M Italian Restaurant

"Accomplishments don't erase shame, hatred, cruelty, silence, ignorance, discrimination, low self-esteem or immorality. It covers it up, with a creative version of pride and ego. Only restitution, forgiving yourself and others, compassion, repentance and living with dignity will ever erase the past."

— Shannon L. Alder

Dedication

A HUGE thank you to my readers. All of you inspire me to keep going! Your love of The Cast Iron Skillet Mystery Series and Jolie and her crew (of friends and family) means the world to me. I can't begin to describe how much I've enjoyed getting to know so many of you through social media and our monthly newsletter!

As always, I have to thank my team of people who help me through every step of the process—and it is a long process to write and publish a book. Thanks to Lourdes Venard, who edits my work and helps me get the story right every time! Also, thanks to Rebecca Grubb, who helps to edit my work. I love having you to text and email back and forth almost daily brainstorming and discussing plot! The covers are to die for—no pun intended! Karen Phillips does amazing work on the covers, and I love the collaborative relationship she and I share. Other people I always have in my corner are Steven and Linda Rath, Merry B, Rosie W, Michelle W, Mary Ann W, and Susanna G who all read the final draft one last time to help locate any mistakes I make along the way. Speaking of that, any mistakes found in the book fall on my shoulders as the author. I have to thank the Guppies who give me sage advice and remain a positive influence throughout my writing career.

Lastly, I thank my family and friends. You are all

inspirations to me daily. My husband, Mike, and our cat family that recently went from eight cats to six then grew from six to nine cats. I don't think I will ever believe that I deserve such a blessed life that I have with all of you. The support and belief you have in me are unwavering—BUT the love that overflows is something that nothing can ever take away from any of us.

Chapter One

I have been on a romantic roller coaster ride this past year. I prefer not to think about it, let alone talk about it. Summer is here, and I'm ready to chillax poolside; I adore living in a state where I get to enjoy each season. It makes me feel like I get a fresh start. Unfortunately, Ava won't let my love life rest.

"I still can't believe the shape your love life is in, girl. How do you manage it?" Ava asked, popping a jalapeño into her mouth.

"It's a gift. Those are HOT!" I exclaimed as her beautiful mocha skin turned into bright red blotches and her eyes bulged out of her head.

"Wa...WAT...WATER!!!" she finally managed to spit out, fleeing for the sink.

"No, here, drink this milk instead; it will do more to ease the heat," I said, pouring a glass.

Ava took two big gulps of the eight-ounce glass of milk and began swirling her head left to right in a panic.

"More?" I asked.

She nodded her head. I wasn't even able to pour

a full glass this time before she took the carton of milk from me and began chugging it.

"Slow down. You're going to make yourself sick."

"Why is that deathly hot? I love spicy food, but that is ridiculous!" Ava said.

"I'm trying something new in the jalapeño cheddar cornbread recipe."

"Are you trying to kill people by heat index? Good lord, Jolie, did you bother to taste that before using it?" Ava slammed her fist on the counter.

"Why are you crying?" I asked.

"I'm not crying, you fool; the heat from whatever peppers you used is eating through my body and making all the water pour out of my eyes." She reached for a paper towel to blow her nose.

"Calm down. I'm testing it out. I'm not eating them from the jar like an—" I thought better to finish that statement based on the glare I was getting from Ava. "I'm just saying that I plan to start out using a bit of the juice from the jar and dicing a little up and tasting it in the bread for heat," I said, pivoting in tone.

"Well, you need to have a death label on those things to warn us spicy lovers . . ." Ava stopped midsentence. Her blotchy, red skin was going pale, and she began dry heaving while holding a hand up in a panic.

Ava ran through the kitchen swinging doors to the front of the restaurant where the men's and women's bathrooms were. She grabbed the doorknob to the women's and pushed to no avail, her body smacking into the door hard. It looked like it was occupied. At this point, Ava looked like a chipmunk, with cheeks extended and eyes wide. She looked desperately at the men's room and then didn't hesitate to run into it.

Magda, our new part-time waitress, looked at me shocked. She wasn't used to Ava's antics yet. Last October, our village lost Ellie Siler, my grandma's best friend and one of my favorite women. Magda was recommended to us by Ellie's niece, Betsy, who had taken over her aunt's chocolate store. Ava and I were also able to add two other staff members: Mirabelle, a twenty-four-year-old hostess with the mostess (as Aunt Fern loved to call her) and her sidekick, Spy. Spy was Mirabelle's seeing-eye dog. Mirabelle has Down's syndrome and sight issues. These two were a super duo, greeting each customer as they entered the restaurant.

"I don't understand what I ever saw in you," Bradley said, robotically shuffling out of the men's room and peering down at his clothing, arms, and legs, spread wide with Ava's spicy barf.

She came stomping out after him. "I didn't know you were in there washing your hands. Why didn't you lock the door?"

"Because I just walked in and was planning to be in there for no more than a minute to wash my hands. There aren't many people in here, and none are men. I thought I was safe for a quick minute. I should have known better with you working here, though."

"*Working* here?" Ava scowled.

Oh boy, Bradley had just done himself in. He knew it too. He put his hands up in defense.

"I know, you *co-own* the place—sorry!" he exclaimed.

"Let's take this situation outside please," I said, glancing around at the few customers trying to eat their meals.

Customers had definitely noticed. There were uncomfortable looks and some whispering in the dining room. I suddenly realized I needed to do damage control.

Ladies and gentlemen, due to the current... *condition* of the dining room, I recommend that you take your dining experience to-go. I will box up your food right away. And because of the inconvenience, it is on the house!"

Mirabelle and Spy have been here a bit longer than Magda, so I saw Mirabelle grinning as Spy shifted his seated position. The golden retriever looked like he had a grin on his face too.

After some serious groveling and comping of the bills, Magda and I worked to clean up the mess as quickly as possible, temporarily closing the restaurant while we did so. "Miss Jolie, can Spy and I help?" Mirabelle asked as I turned the sign and locked the door for a bit.

A lot of people treated Mirabelle differently. They gawked or felt sorry for her and acted like she was less in some way. I'm not even sure anyone meant to do it; they didn't seem to understand how to best communicate with her. I used to be the same way until Ava and I took some time over the summer months of high school to coach Special Olympics. We learned how exceptional Mirabelle is at all things.

"Sure thing. Let's see, Magda is cleaning up the men's bathroom and I'm going to do a run-through of the front of the store to make sure everything is clean. I'd like to sweep the floors and wipe down the tables. Which would you like to do?"

"We'll clean tables," Mirabelle squealed in excitement, and I say she squealed because every time Mirabelle was given a task, she was fully excited to conquer it. She had energy and a zest for life that I wish I could mimic. Spy did a soft *woof* in agreement as he always seemed to talk to Mirabelle.

We both jumped as we heard a hard knock on our front door.

Bradley's boss, Lou, was standing outside the door. I unlocked and opened the door briefly. "Sorry, Lou, we had an unfortunate incident a few moments ago. I had to close briefly to clean up. I'll open back up soon."

"Where is Bradley? He wanted me to meet him here, and here I am. Why we can't talk at the workplace is beyond me. This is ridiculous. He could at least be outside regardless of what 'incident' you've had," he said, tight-lipped.

"Bradley was part of the incident. He probably ran to change his clothes. I would assume he'll be back soon." I sighed heavily, crossing my arms.

"Figures. I'll call him," he said, sneering while grabbing his phone and storming off.

As I went to close and lock up again, Mr. and Mrs. Seevers, a lovely elderly couple that I've known my entire life, stormed up to Lou.

"You no-good son-of-a-gun. I oughta take that phone and shove it up your—"

"Earl!" Mrs. Seevers' hand flew to her chest. "No need for that kind of talk ever, regardless of how much of a creep this guy is."

"What are you two talking about?" Lou demanded.

"We know what you did, and you won't get away

with it!" Mr. Seevers seethed.

"You two old bats need to mind your own business. I'm out of here," Lou protested, shuffling backward, hands raised, then stomping off with his phone to his ear, probably calling poor Bradley to chew him out.

"I'll make that man wish he were dead, Bea." Mr. Seevers grabbed his wife's arm and shuffled away.

"Rude," Mirabelle said as I closed and locked the door again.

"Agreed," I said, wondering what was going on with the Seevers, a typically nice retired couple, and Lou.

Chapter Two

After a long, chaotic day dealing with Ava's shenanigans, I was beat and went to bed early. I fell right to sleep. Soft images danced in my mind's eye as my tongue slowly rounded my lips as they parted. My hands moistened; my body trembled. I was in the middle of a lovely, sexy dream that I never wanted to end. My large blue eyes glossed over, and I moaned in pleasure as my mouth moistened, my saliva increasing as I leaned in to allow the ooey-gooey chocolate from the fountain to drizzle into my mouth. I was just getting ready to experience the sugary, rich molten warmth when my cell phone buzzed and startled me out of my tasty dream. I sat straight up like a stiff board, then collapsed, shoulders drooping. My mouth was no longer moist, but bitter—like my mood. There was a bag of marshmallows on the nightstand and I eyeballed it momentarily, drifting back to the dream, dipping the white, puffy...BZZZZZZZ!

"Huh," I mumbled, rubbing my scrunched-up face.

"*Unicorns, rainbows, fire, brimstone,*" the distorted voice whispered.

"Who is this?" I asked, now alert.

No answer. Whoever it was had hung up, I looked at the clock—2:18 A.M. I sat still, thinking about the sinister tone of the distorted voice. Had it been a man or a woman? I had no idea. Goose bumps formed up my arms as I shivered, pulling the comforter tight around me, short breaths bursting in and out. Paranoia was taking over my mind. I shoved the covers back and got up, and in doing so woke the four cats sprawled out all around me. Each of my fur babies began to do their kitty yoga stretches with sleepy eyes. Some showed affection with soft purrs and others gave me the stink face for interrupting their catnaps. We all headed downstairs to the kitchen, my safe haven when the world got too scary.

I loved my country-style kitchen with wooden cabinets that I had painted a meadow green and a dark marble countertop. I put on the teakettle and unhooked one of my smaller cast iron skillets from a hook on the suspended wood plank that hung from the ceiling directly over the center-kitchen island. Next, I grabbed a couple eggs from the fridge and scrambled them while heating up the skillet with butter and a tad bit of cream.

I was monitoring my eggs when my phone rang again. The hairs lifted on the nape of my neck as every muscle in my body tightened. I slowly turned the cell over. It was Ava calling—my innards breathed a sigh of relief as the knots that had formed loosened just as quickly.

"Why are you calling me at three a.m. in the morning?"

"I'm out back and saw your kitchen light on," she said. I looked out the kitchen window to our adjoining backyards. Ava was waving.

"New question, why are you in your backyard at three A.M. woman?"

"My papi goes to work early this morning and has a long day—we try to talk once a week, so he asked that I call him early today, since Ohio and Santo Domingo are an hour's difference. I felt like walking outside to call him and noticed your light on."

"Come on over; I'm fixin' some eggs."

"Hello?" I waited a beat, then heard a knock at the door. Unlocking the door, I exclaimed, "You didn't have to hang up on me!"

"I was coming over, and it took less than thirty seconds to get here. I wasn't fearing for our friendship," Ava said as she tossed her phone on the island, grabbed a glass out of the cabinet, and helped herself to orange juice from the refrigerator. Next, she plopped down on an island stool with her head in her hands.

"You okay?" I asked.

"Yeah, I miss my family since they moved. I never thought I'd miss them this much." The sorrow in Ava's voice did not match her neon green-and-hot pink geometrically shaped cotton short shorts and her electric blue sleeveless tee emblazoned with *Who's Amazing? Right, ME! And Don't YOU Forget it!* in bright yellow, huge letters. They popped out at my tired eyes.

"Sometimes I wish it were my family that had moved instead of yours," I said, swinging around from the stove to give her a knowing look while rolling my eyes.

Ava grinned, knowing I really didn't mean it. My family could be a handful sometimes—no, make that ninety-nine percent of the time.

"Why are you up scrambling eggs?" Ava asked as Bobbi Jo jumped up on the island and sat staring at Ava, reaching a tortoiseshell paw out toward Ava's face with her claws sticking out. Ava jumped back, almost falling off the stool.

"Girl, don't even with me tonight!" Ava bellowed at Bobbi Jo.

"This morning."

"Huh?" Ava gave me a quizzical look.

"It's morning—and she's not going to hurt you! You know that's how she shows affection," I said in defense of my cat.

"Those claws sticking out don't look like she wants to love on me!" Ava screeched. She hesitantly reached her hand out to Bobbi Jo, who put her paw on Ava's hand. These two had a complicated history, but they loved each other.

"Yeah, I was woken from an intense dream when my cell phone rang," I began but was quickly interrupted.

"A naughty dream? Who was it about, Detective Hottie or Keith?"

"It—"

"OR BOTH?" Ava leaned over the island, scooping Bobbi Jo up into her arms as the two looked at me eagerly.

"Neither," I said. Ava opened her mouth to say more but I held up a firm hand and glared, signaling for her to let me speak. "My dream," I held out the word for effect, "was about a chocolate fountain. I was getting ready to eat a marshmallow dipped in chocolate when the phone buzzed—it was a creepy, distorted voice that only said four words before they hung up."

"That's weird," Ava said.

"Tell me about it! Maybe it was some teens doing prank calls?" I suggested.

"I've never seen you eat a marshmallow before."

"Not the point!"

"Sorry, yeah—probably bored kids who found some new app to mess around with," she said, stroking Bobbi Jo from head to her little torti bobtail. "What were the words?"

"Ummm . . ." I mumbled, grabbing an extra plate and plopping the scrambled eggs on our plates and reaching for the ketchup from the fridge. "Fire, unicorns, brimstone—I can't remember the fourth word."

"Morbid sense of humor," she said, shoving a forkful of ketchup-covered eggs into her mouth.

"Rainbows! That was the other word—but they said it in a different order."

"At least there was good stuff in there," she said, munching the rest of her eggs. Ava always woofed her food down while I attempted to enjoy it—then again, it depended on what the food was. Eggs were healthy enough for me to eat slowly—chocolate, pizza, French fries, on the other hand, were a different story.

As we ate, a siren roared by the house. "That's odd to hear in the middle of the night! I hope it's nothing too serious," I said.

Ava headed to the living room to peek out the window. "It was a sheriff," she said.

"Maybe it's the teens who called me. Maybe they're causing more mishaps?"

An ambulance raced past next as I moved next to Ava at my living room window, which looked out on the darkened road. The sirens stopped a little farther down our road. Ava and I moved outside in our pajama shorts and tops with slippers on to get a better look.

"Can you tell what house they are at?" I asked.

"I don't think so," Ava said.

"Others are starting to wake up," I said as we looked around to see lights turning on and curtains being drawn back. Small brick and stone cottages lined my road. Most had tiny well-manicured yards with lush, bright-colored, floral gardens in front; several folks kept vegetable gardens in the backyard—like me. I had no doubt phone calls would be made to others in the village despite the early hours. Our little hamlet thrived on local gossip.

"Wait, where are you going?" I asked, chasing after Ava and knowing darn well what she was doing.

"It's Lou's house, Jolie," Ava said, picking up speed. Lou's cottage was a short two-block walk.

We came up behind the cautionary tape, and I grabbed Ava's arm. Dread spread throughout my body. This was an all-too-familiar feeling from last fall, except we were on the other side of the cautionary tape that morning—and it was light out then—not dusk.

"I hope Lou is okay," I said.

"I don't have a good feeling," Ava said. She pulled out her phone and started texting.

"Who are you texting?"

"Bradley, he'd want to know if something happened to his boss," Ava said. She finished up and then elbowed me in the side.

"Ow," I howled, rubbing my hip bone and giving Ava an injured look.

"What are you two doing out here at this hour?" Detective Meiser appeared at the other side of the tape.

I felt my face blaze with heat but attempted to remain calm. Our relationship had turned into a bumpy ride since we met last fall. Meiser had bid on a date with me for the village's local Best Paws Auction to help local stray animals. He even adopted an adorable one-eyed cat named Stewart.

"The sirens woke us," I said automatically, realizing my lie as soon as it was out of my mouth. Why did I always get flustered around him?

"Cool, Jolie! You are going to turn us into suspects acting like a weirdo," Ava spat out. "We were already up—I was outside on the phone with my dad when I saw Jolie's kitchen light on—she was making eggs after some creepy phone call she got. Next thing we know we hear sirens, and here we are," Ava simply stated. Why was that so difficult for me to do?

Meiser eyeballed me suspiciously. "What kind of creepy phone call?" Did I detect worry in his voice?

"I think it was some teens prank calling. It was a distorted voice, and Ava said they could have been playing around with a new app or something—it was no big deal," I said, brushing it off.

"Why did you lie to me just now?" Meiser asked, his brown eyes intensely looking directly into my soul.

Okay, so not worried. Ava was right—he was now suspicious. "I don't know—I realized what I did as soon as the words came out of my—"

"You make her nervous," Ava blurted, crossing

her arms and glaring at him. "And I believe you know that and probably like that you make her anxious."

Meiser grinned. "You could be correct on that, Ava. Now, unless you two have some pertinent information on what's going on here, I'll have to ask you to leave."

"How would we know what's going on? Why do you think we are here? To find out! So, spill it, Detective!" Ava had a way of grating on Meiser's nerves.

"I'm afraid I can't share that information with you right now," he said through clenched teeth.

"Manswer," Ava mumbled under her breath.

"What was that?" Meiser asked.

"I said 'manswer.' You know, you gave me a typical manswer—not a real answer but a manswer," she harrumphed, putting one hand on her hip and gawking at him.

I thinned my lips out and just shook my head— no words.

Changing the subject, Meiser said, "Nice cat slippers and chocolate bar P.J.s." He eyeballed me up and down. I was in my matching pajama shorts and a tank top that had chocolate bars all over them with my black cat slip-on slippers. Hot face—again!

We were interrupted by the black SUV, the coroner's vehicle, which slowly showed up. Bradley's fire red vehicle came flying up behind the SUV screeching to a halt. Lydia jumped out of the passenger's side running around to follow Bradley.

The two of them had been dating for several months. "What's going on? Why is the coroner here?" Bradley demanded. Wild chunks of thick black hair from leftover product were protruding from his head and his normally clean-shaven boyish face was scruffy, but he had his recorder sticking out toward Meiser's face—always the reporter.

"I'm afraid I can't answer that right now," Meiser said, holding up the tape for Colleen, the village's coroner, to come through. Colleen meekly moved toward the house in her beige pants, off-white button-up shirt, and her dark blonde hair pulled tightly in a bun. First, she stopped to put on plastic booties over her Softspot beige shoes before entering.

Lydia made a move to go under the tape, but Meiser blocked her way as she looked up from her bent-over position. "I'm a nurse, Detective," she said. "I can go in and offer help to the paramedics."

Well-played, I thought to myself.

"There's no need for that," Meiser said, raking his fingers through his hair.

"So, he's dead?" Bradley said, chewing on his lip.

Meiser kept a straight face and turned to go into Lou's home.

Chapter Three

After Meiser insisted Ava and I leave the scene, we decided to head home, change into our work garb, and head in early. On the way to the restaurant, Lydia texted Ava, who was driving. Ava nodded for me to read the text.

Tell your bestie that her boyfriend is hauling Bradley down to the station for questioning right now!!!!! Those two are perfect for each other!

I read the five angry face emojis she added in for effect too.

"Why would he suspect Bradley?" Ava side-eyed me.

Shrugging my shoulders, I texted back:

Why do you think he suspects him?!!!??? I added six angry faced emojis for effect.

Lydia must have predicted this question because her response came at the speed of lightning.

I'm sure Jolie (angry-face, eyeball-roll, steam-blowing-out-of-nose emoji) *had to whisper her two cents into his ear! Why don't you tell her to mind her own business!*

I shook my head and typed:

You just did!!!!!!!! (winky face emoji).

"What is going on? Why is there an entire conversation happening on my phone that I'm not privy to?" Ava complained.

"It's not my fault Lydia won't give me a straight answer!"

Ava had just parallel parked near the restaurant, Cast Iron Creations, that we co-owned. She grabbed her phone, speaking what she was texting.

Was driving, Jolie was texting you. You two need to chill. Now, why did Meiser take Bradley in for questioning? He didn't give a reason?

I was too busy watching Ava text back and didn't notice Lydia had walked right up by my passenger window, arms crossed, glaring down at me. I nearly banged my head as I jumped.

"Good Lord, Lydia, warn a woman why dontcha?" I pushed the door open, causing her to step back.

"Who do you think you are looking at other peoples' text and answering like you are them?" Lydia had large sunglasses on but I could feel those piercing emerald greens of hers staring through me.

"She was driving! When her phone chimed, she gave me the nod to read the text." I rubbed my eyelid and stretched my neck slowly from side to side.

"You could have said it was you! You never take responsibility. It's always been this way with you. Everyone thinks you are *so* wonderful!" Lydia's bleached blonde ponytail bobbed up and down as her perfect body bounced in rhythm with the vexation of each word.

Rolling my eyes, I leaned forward...

Ava had stomped around the car and wedged herself between us. "Enough, you two! I don't care about your childhood squabbles right now. What is going on with Bradley?"

"Meiser told Bradley he found a pink slip with Bradley's name on it." Lydia fumbled with her hands, staring at the ground.

"Wait, *you're* telling me Lou was going to fire *Bradley*?" I asked, mouth gaping open.

"Your detective said he wasn't under arrest officially, but he needed him to go to the station with him to answer some questions. He had the pink slip in a baggie."

"What century was Lou living in? Who uses pink slips to fire anyone anymore?" Ava asked, astounded.

"I don't think that's the point to focus on right now," I said. "Also, he's not *my* detective, Lydia."

"You two are an item now, right?"

"First off, I don't tell him how to do his job! Second, I don't know for sure if we're an item or not," I said, clearing my throat.

Last fall, Mick Meiser showed up in Leavensport for what was only supposed to be a few weeks. His brother, who had been the mayor of Tri-City, sent him here to scope out the village and get a feel for if the small-town folk would be okay with selling off some farmland. Turned out they weren't.

Mick took a liking to our little community and decided to make the move. Soon after his move, his brother resigned as mayor due to alleged attacks on his character about corruption of funds. I'd never found out all the details, but I'd wanted to ask

Meiser a million times.

"How on earth can you *not* know whether you are in a relationship with someone or not?" Lydia pulled her sunglasses down, eyeing Ava knowingly.

Ava shrugged her shoulders.

"I don't enjoy the silent strong-arming going on here." I pointed, jerking my arm back and forth between them.

"She's your best friend," Lydia said with a smirk.

"They are figuring it out, Lydia. You and Bradley couldn't stand each other last fall and look at the two of you now!" *Finally,* Ava defended me.

Lydia shoved her sunglasses back up, turned to a forward march, and soldiered off without another word.

Even with everything that had taken place in a few short hours, we still got to work earlier than normal. I headed back to my kitchen paradise to begin testing the dinner special for the night. I was excited to use the cast iron Dutch oven to make a pork loin dinner. Cooking, baking, messing around with recipes to come up with ways to use the cast iron cookware were my absolute favorite things to do. I swear I could live in a kitchen twenty-four/seven. It also helped to calm my nerves.

While I was gathering all the ingredients, I thought back to last fall's Best Paw Auction. Annually, the town raises money for the strays that show up. Later, we do an auction—everyone chips in something to auction off. The money goes to spay or neuter the strays and get their shots, so people are more likely to adopt them. My family decided to auction me off for a date. Meiser and Keith bid on me; Meiser won.

I kept making excuses for why I couldn't go on a date—holidays, work, broken pipes in the house, car repairs—you name it, I used it as an excuse. Then, he surprised me with a weekend spa retreat for Valentine's Day—I actually went. It was a disaster—no exaggeration—we found a severed hand in the parking lot on our way to check in. Go figure!

Again, I tried to accuse him of trapping me for the weekend. When that didn't work, I tried to hightail it out of there. Ended up we never got our date. We did solve the mystery though, which brought us back to Leavensport. Since then, we've become closer with time. Nothing like a severed body part to bring people together.

Carlos, the only other cook I allowed in the kitchen, came in for his shift.

"Hey, Carlos! I messed with the pork recipe. Altered it a bit—wrote it all down there and got all the ingredients ready to go for you to work your magic." We did our normal high five and I went up front to discuss the pork special with Ava, but she looked dismayed. "You okay?"

"Things are changing. It's not even been a year and there is a second possible murder? My family's moved. When did we become adults?" Ava shook her head.

"I remember when we were planning this restaurant and it was a pretend dream. Something we did as kids. Now, it's a reality." I gazed around the dining room in awe. "I can't believe Lou's gone. Even though he was a curmudgeon, he was consistent."

"True! You need to work your magic and find out if Detective Hottie seriously is considering Bradley as a suspect."

"He won't tell me. Too straitlaced. The Seevers were not happy, to say the least, with Lou yesterday when you were changing clothes." I thought back to the ugly encounter.

"Those two wouldn't hurt a fly," Ava said.

"Are you up for some snooping to find out what's going on?"

Ava's brow furrowed as she gave me a curt nod. We were shaking on it when Ava's girlfriend, Delilah, walked in.

"Hey, babe, what's up?" Ava leaned across the counter to give her girlfriend a peck on the cheek.

Delilah was lugging a large canvas tote that had textile fabrics in Van Gogh-style colorful swirls. She ran the village's arts and craft store—Delilah made all her clothes and bags. She also painted a beautiful mural of the village on one of our walls when we opened a couple of years ago.

"I want to order the jalapeño cheddar cornbread for the Dotting the Eyes art event I'm having at the studio. Actually, I'll order three of them. It's next week on Friday evening," Delilah said. She grabbed her ringing phone. "Can you hold on a minute, please?" she told the caller, then turned back to Ava. "Can you please just jot that down and I'll pay whatever it costs. I'll come to pick it up that Friday around four." She turned to smile at me and walked off.

"What's going on there?" I asked, hoping Ava wouldn't bite my head off. Generally, Delilah was warm and caring. She was one of the few people I knew who would ignore her phone to focus on the people in front of her.

"I don't know—she's not been herself lately, and

she gets upset when I ask her what's wrong," Ava said, biting back tears.

Now I knew it must be serious. I'm an emotional roller coaster who will cry when Spy gives me a cute look. Ava, on the other hand, only shows one emotion: bold, sassy, high-energy. I could count on one hand the times I had seen her cry. I reached over to rub her shoulder, but she shrugged me away and moved toward a table of guests to chat with them.

Meiser walked into the restaurant at that moment and moved toward me. He looked over at Ava and nodded at her, then gave me a concerned look. "What's wrong with her?" he asked.

"What makes you ask that? She said hi."

"Exactly. Normally she's giving me grief or a look of dissatisfaction," he said.

This was true. "I don't know; I think something is going on between her and Delilah, but I don't know what," I said, realizing I should have kept my big mouth shut.

"What don't you know?" Ava said, walking up with an order in hand. She yelled it back through the open window behind our counter to Carlos and then turned to Meiser and me.

"Meiser's still bugging me for that date. He wanted to know if it would soften the blow if we went on a double date with you and Delilah. I told him I didn't know what you'd think," I said. Man, I was a little too good at coming up with lies on the fly. I might need to be concerned!

Meiser gave me an amused look as Ava rubbed her chin, pinching her lips slightly. "Yep—she's right," he said. "What do you say? Double date?"

"I guess. I'll text Delilah to see what she thinks,

and we'll get back to you," Ava said, reaching for her phone. While texting, she said, "You both realize you're equally pathetic, right? The fact you can't make a simple date work says a lot about how alike you both are!"

Meiser and I gave each other a knowing look—yep, Ava was feeling better.

Chapter Four

Since Carlos was finishing up the pork dish, I decided to head over to M&M's Italian Restaurant. It was the lunch hour when I arrived. I purposely planned my visit to see what kind of crowd they pulled at lunch. It seemed sparse. The building and view were truly spectacular. It had a cute awning with the Italian colors of green, white, and red outside and a few tables under it. The view looked out into vast fields of yellow and green, as well as the woods set in the back. They had a deep, dark wood-covered patio in the back of the restaurant. The Zimmerman brothers and their wives were seated out front, eating what looked to be a decadent, hearty helping of spaghetti and meatballs with thick slices of bread and a garlicy aroma that made my mouth drool.

I drew in a deep breath as I strolled inside. There were brick walls and dark, square wooden frames outlined the entire ceiling. Arches throughout the restaurant had lifelike vines of greens, and grapes spiraled around the arches and hung from the framed wooden ceiling. Whoever did their decorations had a great eye. A sleek woman with a short, black bob came gliding up to me in a short black dress with blood-red high heels. "Welcome to M&M's Italian Restaurant. Will there just be one today?" She smiled brightly.

"I'm not eating in today. I'd love to take a look at your menu, though, if you don't mind. I have never been in here before. It took my breath away how beautiful the building is," I said, looking around.

"Thank you. My sister, Star, will be delighted to hear that. She decorated the restaurant and helps me run it. I'm Olive Santorini. Are you local?" she asked, reaching for my hand.

I shook her hand. "Yes, I co-own Cast Iron Creations on the other side of the village near the community center. I'm Jolie Tucker."

"Your hair is beautiful! Blonde and curly—is that natural?" She eyed my hair.

"I wish it were natural. My best friend, Ava—who also co-owns the restaurant with me—has naturally curly hair. I've always been jealous, so I started getting perms at a young age. She works to straighten her hair, though. Go figure, right?" I said, grinning at her.

She smiled as she grabbed a leather menu to hand over to me. "Yes, Star has natural curls too but straightens it. We always want what we can't have."

"So true."

"Wait, is Ava's girlfriend the art teacher, Delilah?"

"Yes."

"I adore her! She works with my daughter, Gaze." Olive laid her perfectly manicured hand over her heart.

"Delilah is wonderful at what she does," I had to agree.

"I'm sorry, we don't have takeout menus to send home with people yet. That is next on my list, though. You are welcome to look through the menu, and I hope you will come back to join us soon," she said as another couple came in to be seated.

I moved over to the bar and sat to look through the menu, waiting for her to come back so I could ask about maybe doing some cross-selling. Betsy, a friend who now owns Chocolate Caper, and I have been working to cross-sell products in our village with local merchants. I'd love to help sell that garlic bread and maybe some cannoli and zeppolis too. Their dessert menu looked yummy, but all things with sugar looked great to me.

Another striking woman with short, thick wavy black hair came up to the bar. She had the same languid walk as Olive. "Hello, you must be Star!" I said.

The woman looked at me skeptically, as if trying to place me. "Yes," she said hesitantly. "And who are you?"

"I'm so sorry; I'm Jolie Tucker. You don't know me. I just spoke to your sister a minute ago and I took a guess because you two look alike and she mentioned you have naturally curly hair that you try to straighten and your hair is beautiful, but it is wavy, like someone who would try to straighten it." I said all of that in one quick breath and realized how clumsy I was in social situations.

Star looked exhausted listening to me, but she kindly reached across the dark mahogany bar to shake my hand. "Yes, I wish I could get it straighter, but this is the best I can do," she said, blushing as she fluffed her hair. "Can I get you a drink?"

"Hey, I see you met Jolie. She runs that cute little restaurant, Cast Iron Creations, over by the art district," Olive said, walking up to take a seat next to me.

"Oh yeah, I keep meaning to stop in and try something there. Our chef does a few dishes with cast iron," Star said.

"So, are you two the co-owners of this restaurant then?" I asked. I had tried to figure out who owned this place for some time now. The two women gave each other a strange look, then Olive said, "Nope, not the owners. We manage and take care of everything for the owner, though."

I noticed she didn't share a name. "Oh, okay— my friend Betsy now owns Chocolate Capers. The two of us have been doing a lot of cross-selling of our products. We are expanding that idea throughout the village, and I dropped by today to see who owned the restaurant to see if they would be interested in cross-selling any products. It's a great opportunity for all of us to drum up more business while supporting each other," I said, making my routine spiel.

"We've been fortunate to do pretty good business for just opening up. We are getting a lot of traffic coming from the city, and many locals are coming to try our daily specials," Star said, glancing at her sister.

"Wowser," I said, looking at the menu. "Twenty dollars for spaghetti and meatballs!" I couldn't help but exclaim, "I *have* to try any pasta that cost that much." I tend to speak without thinking and often put my foot in my mouth. The problem is I'm reflective enough to know as soon as the words spill out of my mouth, like right now.

The sisters looked at each other uncomfortably. "It's an old family recipe from the owner's great-grandmother from Naples. It is truly out of this world—especially those meatballs," Olive said.

"Yes, and we haven't had any issues selling it or complaints on the price yet," Star lifted her chin, nostrils flaring.

"I'm sorry, that wasn't a nice comment. I tend to put my—" I was interrupted by Mr. Seevers, who walked up to us.

"Hello, dolls," he said, taking a seat next to me.

"Hi, Mr. Seevers, how are you?" I asked, relieved for the save.

"Well, I never got my morning coffee yet, but no one got hurt—so I'd say, 'pretty good' at this point in time." He grinned widely.

Olive took a cue and grabbed a coffee mug and pot of coffee. "Let's keep you happy then," she said.

Mr. Seevers put his hand over the mug and said, "Don't suppose you have a to-go cup, do ya? I was stopping in to make a reservation for me and the better half's anniversary that is coming up."

Meanwhile, another couple came into the restaurant. Olive asked Star to run back for a to-go cup while she seated the couple who had just walked in.

"Sorry you had to hear that ruckus the other day outside your restaurant," Mr. Seevers said.

"What was that all about? I'm not used to seeing you get so angry," I asked.

"Lou swindled us out of a bunch of money!" Mr. Seevers beat his fist against the bar and I jumped on my stool. "Sorry, young lady, I worked hard to earn my retirement. Lou was doing a side job in investments. I've known him since he was in diapers. He reached out to most of the seniors who live in the village with a 'can't fail' investment opportunity. I suppose we were all a little to blame for believing him, but we all know each other here."

"I had no idea he was moonlighting another job. I'm so sorry that happened to you. Did everyone who invested lose money?" I asked.

"Yep, I and the Zimmerman brothers lost the most from it, though. Bea is thinking of getting a part-time job, but I told her not to worry about it. We're looking to downsize now and sell our house and property. I think we'll do fine if we can get a price for our land. But the Zimmermans—they've owned that farmland for generations. You thought *I* was mad!"

"Oh no, they aren't going to have to sell the farm, are they?"

"I hope not, but I wouldn't doubt it. I'm not going to lie to you; I'm not sad at all that Lou kicked the bucket, but I wouldn't wish a gruesome murder on anyone," he said, shaking his head.

"So, it was murder?" I asked.

"Yep, it wasn't pretty, from what I hear. Rumor mill says he could have been poisoned and beat to death—although they are still trying to figure out which order it all happened."

Chapter Five

As I walked to my car, I noticed survey flags breaking up pieces of land that surrounded the restaurant. The Zimmerman brothers were finishing up their meal and heading toward me; I was a bit surprised to see them here.

"How are things, Jolie?" Zed asked, toothpick in the mouth. He and his brother were wearing their denim bib overalls with work boots. Both had long grayish beards that hung to their chest, and both had ponytail holders in their beards today with long dark brownish-gray hair held in ponytails on the back.

"Can't complain. I hadn't been inside this place before and was stopping to see if they may want to do some cross-selling, but the sisters didn't seem interested," I said.

"We hadn't been either. Walked inside and knew we best sit outside with our farm gear on. Not used to fancy places like this," Zander said. "Good food, but too pricey for my taste."

"Yeah, twenty dollars for spaghetti and meatballs. I have to admit, I'm tempted to try it, though," I said, feeling vindicated that some of the villagers agreed about the price. The truth is, people in our village would never complain about the price to the managers, but they'd sure enough gossip about it behind their backs—kind of like I was doing now. I found it strange to hear the Zimmermans had to sell their land, yet they could afford an expensive lunch.

"Is some of this land yours?" I asked, pointing to the fields marked off to sell.

"Yeah, we got land all different places around the village. I suppose you heard we lost some money with Lou's investment scheme. We're trying to keep as much land as we can. We heard that there are others in the city interested in buying land around this restaurant. The highway goes straight to the city—I think they're hoping to get city folk to come here for a down-home, small-town feel," Zed said, nodding his head toward the highway.

"You know, now that you mention it, last fall Nancy from the police station was talking about urban sprawl happening in our village. I didn't take it seriously at the time," I said.

"What's that?" Zander said, putting a wad of chew in his mouth.

"Seems like it's what you just said is happening here. We have our highway, which goes into the city—but it's a ways away. We got this restaurant here, now more of the land is being sold. Someone wants to buy up the land—the fields and woods between here and the city—and make money. At some point, we'll be part of the city. It's nothing illegal, though," I said. I needed to figure out who owned this restaurant. That would be the first step in figuring out if my theory was correct or not. "Do either of you know who owns this place?"

"Nope, and I'll tell you something. I won't be back after hearing that. It sounds like old Lou could have had his hand in getting some of the money from this sprawl," Zed said. "Good thing someone thought to off him."

"We need to head back to the farm, Zed. I think we should try to figure out another way to save our land. I don't want no city folk comin' and takin' over here," Zander said, spitting a disgusting-looking wad on the sidewalk by the patio. The two walked away, heads together, planning their next move.

I turned to go to my car, feeling a bit unsettled by all the resentment in the air, and noticed that Star was standing at the door. I couldn't be sure how much she heard, but she did not look happy with me. I gave a half-grin and waved but got a glare and her back in return. Again, I felt it would have been better to keep my big mouth shut. For someone who likes to be alone and desires quietude, I sure do have a big mouth.

I headed for the center of the village to the courthouse to see if I could access records to find out who the owner was. On my way, I called Ava to see how things were going at the restaurant.

"Delilah said she'd go on a double date," Ava said, sounding deflated.

"That doesn't sound promising," I said.

"Well, I don't know what to tell you, Jolie. She said she'd do it. You asked, and now it's happening. Things are fine here; gotta go."

She hung up. Obviously, things were not fine. Great, Meiser and I finally go on a date, and Ava and Delilah have some feud brewing. And double great, now I feel like a colossal jerk for caring more about my date with Meiser than what was going on with Ava.

I had to circle the block a few times to find a spot on the street near the courthouse. I got out of my car as Bea Seevers came out of the police station next door. "Hi, Mrs. Seevers," I said, almost saying I had just seen her husband at M&M's. But I bit my tongue as I remembered he was making reservations for their anniversary.

"Hi," she said, moving quickly by me.

"Are you okay?" I asked, swinging around.

She stopped and turned. "Not really, dear. Seems Mr. Seevers and I and a whole host of other elderly villagers who decided to trust that no-good son-of-a—" She paused, turning her head away as she brushed angry tears from her eyes." Lou—we are all considered suspects in his murder. They are calling us all in to give statements."

"Oh, no! I'm sorry. Can I do anything to help?"

"Yeah, you can find the person who murdered him, like you did last autumn. We could use a young villager on our side." She grabbed my hand, patting it.

"Seems Bradley is a suspect too," I said. "I plan on doing some investigating."

Ava talked way more than I did. Why wasn't she ever the one to make promises on finding murderers? I didn't actually promise her, did I? I was trying to relive the moment with Mrs. Seevers, wondering how serious she was about me finding the killer, as I walked in and saw Margy at the desk of the courthouse.

Margy was a hoot. She had to be in her seventies,

and she kept her hair buzzed after a stint with
cancer—but she always had bright red, purple, blue,
or multiple-colored hair with large framed bright
pink eyeglasses and tons of makeup.

Today, she was sporting bright red hair with
shades of blue running through. "Whatcha need,
dollface?" she asked as she chomped on her gum.

"Hey, Margy. Are you able to tell me if it is a
public record for me to see who owns a restaurant
in town?"

"Of course, that's public record," she said.

"Do I just give you the name or do I look it up
online? I have no idea how to go about it."

"You can look it up online by typing in the
business name and generally, if there is a website, it
will be listed in the 'about' section. You can also
search the Better Business Bureau, but since you're
here, I can look it up for you."

"Thanks, I'm looking for who owns the new
M&M's Italian restaurant in town."

"Oh, great food. Too expensive for our village,
though."

I grinned. "I haven't tried it yet, but I will
someday."

"Have a seat; I'll be right back with your info,"
she said, grabbing a file to take back with her. I
noticed all five-foot-two of her had on black leather
pants with an off the shoulder gray eighties-looking
sweatshirt that had bright geometric shapes
covering it. She seemed to buy her clothes from
Hang Tight Clothes for Teens—not what one would
expect for a woman of her age working at the
courthouse. I had to say she made it work.

My phone vibrated and I saw Keith had texted

me a few minutes ago.

I'm at the police station. I saw your car parked out front. Are you around?

Keith and I had a history. We grew up together and went to high school together, where we dated. He was a jock; I have nothing against people who play sports, even though I am not gifted in athletics. He wanted things to work out more than I did. I have trust issues with men, which is one reason it was now summer, and I still hadn't been on a real date with Mick.

I'm over at the courthouse waiting on Margy to pull a file for me.

I looked down at my phone, waiting for a reply, only to see out of the corner of my eye Keith walk in the door. He looked great as always in his worn jeans, tennis shoes, and a tight-fitting tee.

"Don't tell me Teddy thinks you're a suspect for Lou's murder?" I asked.

"Nah, he's having a rough day having to call many of the elderly from the village."

"Did you hear about Bradley?"

"I heard the detective suspected him." Keith stared at his hands tight-lipped.

"Supposedly, Lou was going to fire him? Did you know about that? Did Bradley know?" I bombarded him with questions.

"Bradley had not been happy with Lou for some time. Every time I asked him about it, he'd brush it off as *work stuff.*"

"Maybe Bradley did know it was coming," I said more to myself than Keith.

"I wouldn't think you'd automatically side with the detective. Teddy seems more focused on someone who had lost money. He's not enjoying having to grill his elders, so I stopped by Cast Iron Creations and picked up some of your berry crumble cake to bring to him. Ava did not seem like she was in a good mood."

"She and Delilah seem to be having a rough patch," I said. As an afterthought, I added, "I hope she isn't rude to all the customers."

"So, it's okay if she's rude to me?" he asked in a teasing way.

"You know what I mean!"

"I'm kidding! I'm sure she's fine with everyone else. We all get to take out our aggressions on the ones we grew up with and are most comfortable with," he said, brushing my shoulder with a playful fist.

"Jolie, I wrote down the information you were looking for," Margy said, trotting out from back and handing over an envelope.

"Thanks, Margy."

"What's that about?" Keith asked.

"Just something I'm looking into."

"Are you going to the town meeting tonight?" he asked.

Not being able to control my urge to find out who the owner was, I tore the envelope open and stared at the page. "I forgot about it—but after getting this information—I will be there."

Chapter Six

I had time to stop back at the restaurant before heading home to change for the meeting. Mirabelle and Spy greeted me as I walked in.

"Hi, welcome to Cast Iron Creations, where we put the comfort in comfort food!" Mirabelle squeaked in glee. Spy gave a sweet *wolf* while wagging his tail.

"Well now, that's a new greeting," I giggled.

"Ava helped me come up with it! Carlos loves it too!" Mirabelle clapped. Carlos's naturally sweet personality made him Mirabelle's favorite. I tried not to be jealous.

I looked at a grinning Ava in her black tights, lime green mini, and red checkered shirt. Ava's hands popped up in the air. "She wanted a snazzy welcoming line. It was all her idea—don't look at me!"

"Well, I love it! It is so much more personal than a simple hello." I rubbed Spy on his head.

Mirabelle had a gleam in her soft hazel eyes.

Magda had come in for her afternoon shift, so I waved a hand for Ava to follow me back to our office.

"Hey, Carlos! Smells delicious!"

"You did all the footwork. Adding the pork loin to the one-dish gnocchi, beans, and greens was very smart."

I smiled, picked up a testing spoon, closed my eyes to inhale the mix of garlic, oregano, and bacon, and let the flavors burst around my taste buds. I opened my eyes wide, nodding vigorously.

"Girl, leave some for the customers," Ava interrupted.

"Sorry," I said, giving Carlos a thumbs-up, then moving into the cramped office to shut the door.

"What's so private?" Ava asked.

I moved her to one side while I sat at the desk, pulling up a slide software program.

"Are we presenting something?"

"We're both visual people," I said, connecting my phone to the computer.

"K . . ." Ava contemplated.

I scrolled through my pictures and dropped a picture of M&M's Italian Restaurant in one slide. Next, I found an old picture of the Zimmerman brothers, one of the Seevers, and one of Bradley, and put each on a slide. I jotted down notes under each picture I entered onto a slide.

Under the picture of the Zimmermans I wrote notes *loss of money, selling farmland.*"Are you going to explain?" Ava demanded.

"Today, I met the co-managers of M&M's. They wouldn't tell me who the owner is, so I did some digging. Also, I saw the Zimmerman brothers at M&M's eating an expensive lunch, yet Lou swindled their family out of a lot of money, and they have to sell some land. Don't you find that strange?"

"Yeah, Bradley came in earlier while you were out," Ava said as an afterthought.

"He did, so they aren't holding him?"

"Nope, he was not happy. Lydia was with him. I think she was hoping to get her grip around your neck!"

"That's an unpleasant thing to say! Why were they both so angry if he wasn't being held?"

"I think Lydia still thinks you put a bug in Meiser's ear. Bradley seemed angry at the world. He couldn't believe Lou was going to fire him. He was hot under the collar about Meiser's questions too. I guess his alibi was Lydia, but he said Meiser told him not to leave town," Ava said.

"Meiser's just doing his job. Hmmm...I had a theory that maybe Bradley knew he was going to be fired though. Guess I got that wrong."

"Well, the two of them were pretty irate. I will say that Bradley seemed genuinely surprised to find out that Lou was going to fire him." Ava reached for the mouse, clicking through to Bradley's picture.

I began typing some notes below each slide.

Under Bradley's picture, *Lou was getting ready to fire him. Only alibi is Lydia.*

"Can't Hide from the Slides!" Ava exclaimed.

My fingers stood frozen over the keyboard as I wrinkled my forehead, staring at Ava sideways.

"That can be the name of our investigation tool!" Ava exclaimed.

"How about we just focus on solving who murdered Lou, and come up with a cute, catchy name later?" I went back to typing.

"Why the picture of M&M's?" Ava asked.

"I'm not sure yet. I feel like it's at the center of a lot of things. Yet I can't explain why."

M&M's picture, *Tri-City, suspicious sisters' as management, mysterious owner.*

"You heard what happened to Lou, right? You can't seriously think that either of the Seevers is capable of beating that man?" Ava jerked her head back.

"I saw Mr. Seevers today and he made an odd comment." I began typing notes by their picture.

Under the Seever's picture I typed, *swindled out of retirement money. Bea Seevers has to get a part time job.*"What was that?"

"He is the one who told me what happened to Lou, but he said that the police can't figure out what order things happened in."

"Weird, so you think one of them poisoned him and the other beat him after he was dead?"

"I don't want to think anything. I definitely don't want to believe anyone in our village could murder another. But hey, I never would have thought Lou would swindle people out of money or that we would have had a murder last year!"

Chapter Seven

It had been a hot day in Leavensport, so I decided to run home to change clothes before the village meeting. I was so intent on creating something that Ava and I could use to help us solve the case that I forgot to remind her about tonight's meeting. I called her to refresh her memory and let her know there wouldn't be a lot of traffic at the restaurant tonight. The monthly meetings brought most folks to it—especially a lot of our regulars.

I grabbed the mail and threw it on the coffee table by the couch for later and ran up the steps to take a quick cold shower to cool off and change. I almost fell over one of the cats' rattle balls in the middle of the hallway. Sammy Jr. came peeking out from under the bed to be sure it was me—he was a one-person kind of cat—and when he saw me, he sauntered over.

"Hey, Juju Bean," I said, using my affectionate kitty voice and calling him by one of his many nicknames. I threw the ball, and my long-haired black beauty went flying after it. He seemed so shy at times but was a major character.

I was stripping down out of my sticky cast iron tee-shirt I had on when the phone rang. I ran over to the bedroom to grab it.

"Hello?"

"Yes, is this Mrs. Tucker?" a woman asked in a raspy voice.

"Yes, this is Miss Tucker."

"Excuse the mistake, ma'am, Miss Tucker, this is Tonya Morrison with the mayor's office in Tri-City. How are you today, ma'am?"

The mayor's office? Was this a prank? "I'm fine," I said hesitantly.

"Mayor Cardinal would like to set up a meeting to meet with you. It will not take long. Does Monday morning at ten work for you?"

"May I ask what this is concerning? I run a restaurant and will need to discuss this with my co-owner." I didn't want to be rude, but I was a bit frustrated to receive this call out of nowhere with no explanation, throwing a date and time at me.

"He'd like to discuss some future opportunities with you. I am going to put you down for Monday at ten and you can call me back at 555-2730 if you need to reschedule. I'm sorry; I need to take another call."

Opportunities? That—was—annoying!

I quickly showered, changed, fed the cats, and threw the unopened mail in my brown leather tote as I headed out.

I pulled into the community center parking lot right as my family did. My Uncle Wylie practically sprinted from the front seat of the car, looking petrified.

"What's wrong, Uncle Wylie?"

"Patty didn't feel like driving. I said I'd do it, but Fernie grabbed the keys before I could get them."

Aunt Fern had no regard for the law when she drove. None of us could believe she still possessed a driver's license.

"You talking to your Uncle Wooly, Jolie?" Aunt Fern asked, giggling. When I was little, I couldn't pronounce the 'y' and called him Uncle Wooly. I still had a bit of Southern twang, and sometimes it still came out as Wooly—and my family wouldn't let me forget it.

"I'm going to be sick," my mom said, moving toward the building with bags full of food. One of the perks of the monthly meetings was everyone brought food, and when the business was all taken care of, it turned into more of a social gathering. This was part of the reason why I had told Ava there wouldn't be too many people out tonight—free food and all.

Leavensport Community Center was at the heart of the village. Not only were monthly town meetings held here, but more often than not, the village would hold holiday gatherings here for everyone to be able to share. Converge Life and Faith Church leaders would take turns at the gathering, sharing each leader's story about their faith with their congregation. We only have one church, so the leaders—pastor, rabbi, priest, pujari, and monks—all share time at the church as they do during holiday seasons. One of the things I loved the most about my hometown is the tolerance that can be found between faiths.

"I'm glad you all brought something. I forgot all about this until Keith reminded me and I had to remind Ava—we didn't make anything this time around. I feel bad."

"You girls always contribute. No one's going to think anything of it. There will be plenty," Grandma Opal said. "Patty, stop being such a drama queen; Fernie was only going twenty miles over the speed limit!"

"She was in a twenty-five-mile zone, Mom—I know that's not fast, but I was waiting to hear sirens!"

"Okay, as usual, people are starting to stare. Can we please go in and get the food set up? I have some things I want to talk to you all about before the meeting," I said, putting my hand on the small of my grandma's back to push her inside.

"Child get your hand off me. I'm going! Good grief!" Grandma shuffled in with her delightful wobbly walk.

We walked back to the kitchen area, where Betsy was setting out some yummy chocolate desserts. She had a plate of homemade chocolate caramels with sea salt sprinkled on top, and a triple layer chocolate cake with buttercream frosting that had chocolate drizzled all over it. After Betsy lost her Aunt Ellie last fall, Betsy had been unhappy working as a nurse. Her aunt, who owned Chocolate Capers, had left the shop to Betsy, who took it over and had done some astounding things her first year. Betsy and I were alike in that we loved to experiment with different recipes.

When Betsy and I had discussed cross-selling we had no idea all the paths it would take us down. For instance, Violet, who ran Vintage Violet's shop in the mall, and Delilah teamed up with Betsy to make a mock chocolate shoe that had all the delicacy of the vintage pumps Violet had shipped in for her shop. Delilah helped by sketching the shoe and helping Betsy manage the lace and molding. Betsy used it for advertising and to bring in more customers.

"That looks amazing," I said. "Don't suppose you need someone to test it out to make sure it's safe for everyone to eat?" I put my purse on the counter. Betsy laughed. "Only because it's you, Jolie!" She cut a small sliver and handed me a plate with a fork. "Now, if it's poisoned, though, you will wish you never tried it," she continued with a hearty chuckle.

"I'll chance it." I took a big bite and moaned in sheer pleasure. "I can sell some at the restaurant for you next week if you want to make some—bring some flyers over from your store too!"

"Of course! I played with your cast iron mole sauce and added some darker chocolate and used it on ice cream. People loved it, and I gave out your flyers. I'll get the recipe to you tomorrow because you will probably be getting some requests for it!"

I loved this cross-selling thing!

"You two might want to keep it down over here, talking about poison," Detective Meiser said as he walked up and grabbed a plate, piling cheese and crackers on it.

"Why are you listening in on our conversation?" I flirted. Then, I saw his expression was deadly serious.

"I'm not kidding," he said.

I tilted my head to the side and pursed my lips. What was his problem?

"I can't say anymore," Meiser said, popping a cracker with a huge chunk of cheddar in his mouth. I saw Bradley moving toward us out of the corner of my eye.

"Lou was poisoned. Someone switched out his blood pressure pills with poison. That was the cause of death." Bradley took two wide steps, then leaned forward, brushing past Meiser to grab cheese and crackers.

Meiser choked on his cracker. "How do you know that?"

"What do you mean? You're the one who thinks I killed him, right?" Bradley snapped.

Meiser's face turned red but as he began a comeback Betsy's face lost all color. She stopped midway into cutting another slice of cake and said, "That's horrible."

I'm sure all of this was bringing back memories of her aunt's murder last year.

Meiser and Bradley both took this a cue to lay off each other.

I rubbed her back and looked at Meiser. "I've heard the rumors about Lou and his financial fraud—some sort of investments that didn't go well and lots of our elderly villagers lost lots of money."

"How do you know all this, Jolie?" Meiser asked.

Bradley came to my rescue. "Including Lou. I don't think he purposely meant for people to lose their money. Someone scammed him but made him the scapegoat. Seems like the police needs to be trying to figure out where all this began."

"It's already out there," Ava said, coming up behind us and putting a few warmers on the counter.

"You made food?" I asked.

"You know I didn't make food," she bellowed. "I had Carlos cook up some cast iron jalapeño cheddar cornbread as a side dish. He told me you perfected the recipe. Plus, he sent the leftover pork loin thingy. I forget what he called the dish."

"Yum," Betsy said, pulling one of the spicy, steaming cornbreads out of the bag and cutting herself a piece. She chomped on it, her bright green eyes lighting up and widening, while her red-haired ponytail bobbed up and down in satisfaction.

Meiser moved to cut a piece. "What's out there?"

"People were talking today in the restaurant about how Lou died and speculating if he lost money," Ava said, cutting a piece of Betsy's cake.

"What I need to find out is who is the person who finds all this information in this town?" Meiser scratched his neck slowly.

"Hey, do you know for sure that Lou was working for someone who scammed him?" I asked, changing the subject.

"We've got a good lead, and *that* is all you will get out of me," he said, popping a bite of cornbread in his mouth. "This is one my favorite things; you need to keep it on the menu! I love spicy food—why didn't I get any of the test batches?"

"That explains why you like my BFF; she's pretty spicy," Ava said, elbowing me in the side and waggling her eyebrows at my flaming face. "Trust me; you didn't want any of the test batches. She made it *way* too fiery!"

I was not a pretty cook. I'd never get a show on the Food Network. My food was good, but it generally took me many test tries before it was ready to serve at our restaurant. Meiser choked a bit on his snack. "Why do you ask?" He subtly changed the topic back to my question.

"I'm planning on bringing up some news I found

out about today at the courthouse. It's odd, and I wondered if the land going up for sale leading to the city has something to do with this investment," I said, grabbing the envelope from my large tote. The mail I had shoved in earlier fell all over the floor.

Ava, Meiser, Betsy, Bradley, and I bent down to grab it. "Was this in your mail?" Ava asked. She handed me a bright red envelope with nothing on it.

"It had to be. I hadn't gotten the mail in a couple of days, so nothing else was sitting on my table when I grabbed the stack. I planned to paw through it during the meeting tonight," I said, reaching for the envelope.

"Someone had to stick it in your box," Meiser said.

I opened the mysterious red envelope and froze.

What looked to be magazine cutouts made out the words, "_unicorns, rainbows, fire, brimstone._" But this time there was more to the cryptic message, "_Mind your business or, witch, you'll be dead!_"

"What is it?" Meiser asked, trying to grab it out of my hands.

I pulled the letter back and stuffed it in my tote. Mayor Nalini was beckoning everyone to enter the main room to begin the meeting.

"It's nothing. Let's go to the meeting."

Meiser, Ava, Bradley, and Betsy gave each other questioning looks.

Chapter Eight

All the usual suspects were in attendance for our monthly meeting: my family, Chief Tobias, Keith, Lydia, Bradley, and Delilah. I saw the Zimmerman crew in back with the Seevers, huddled together, along with about two hundred other villagers. When I was a kid, the community center was smaller; as the village grew, they added onto it. One thing that never changed was that however many more people moved into the village, it continued to be a strong community that was actively involved in the town goings-on.

I opted to sit in the middle of the room. Mayor Nalini was one of those mayors who ran two consecutive terms, then took four years off to run again. He had decided it was time to expand the center during his first term. He wanted the main room to have a raised stage with a lectern and gavel for him to preside over. He looked down on us—a beautiful expanse of faux marble floors with wooden benches spread out in rows. Delilah and her clients did a lot of the artwork in warm colors of rust and dark greens against dark wooden pillars and pews. They made the space inviting and warm.

I had brought a plate of food into the meeting with me, like most villagers, but I set it aside now, not hungry. The note had shaken me. I should have shared the message with the others, but I wasn't in the mood to be the center of attention again. I did think to grab a baggie to put the letter in as to not get more fingerprints on it. At some point, I would share it with Meiser or Chief Tobias to see if they could get any prints off of it.

I was staring off into space when Ava elbowed me from the left side, and Aunt Fern elbowed me from the right side.

"OUCH!" I exclaimed, looking up to see my grandma, who had turned around and was giving me the evil eye. My mom just rolled her dark eyes in embarrassment. "What?" I squealed, a little too loudly.

"The mayor is calling on you, Jolie. Get it together!" Grandma Opal huffed, turned around, and crossed her arms, short gray curls bouncing left to right.

"I'm sorry, sir. What was it you asked again?" I asked, feeling like a turtle entering my shell as all eyes turned to me.

Mayor Nalini was born in India, but his parents moved to our village soon after his birth. He grew up here and became fascinated with US politics. His family was in politics in India. He must have colored his hair because there was no longer any gray in it, but now his thick black hair was combed over to the side with his crisp white button-up shirt and blue tie done perfectly. "The topic of cross-selling is next on the agenda. I believe you and Betsy are heading that up. Can the two of you give us an update, please?"

I looked over and saw that Betsy was standing, waiting for me as well. I hoped she hadn't said anything yet or I'd look even more ridiculous than I already did. "Right now, the majority of shops in the village are participating in one way or another, and it seems to be going well."

Betsy followed up by saying, "Fred's Farm Market, Costello's Grocery, Make Yourself at Home B&B, Kwani's food mart, the school, the hospital, No Cones About It, my shop, and Jolie and Ava's restaurant are all participating at some level at this point and time."

I nodded in confirmation. "I did stop by M&M's Italian Restaurant and spoke to both of the ladies who are managing it. They did not seem interested in cross-selling." I looked around to see if Star or Olive were present at the meeting but didn't see either of them. "I went to the courthouse to find out who owned the restaurant; it's a Mr. Milano. Does anyone know who that is?" I asked.

"Why would you go snooping around to find that out?" Zed Zimmerman boomed with his gravelly voice from the back of the room.

I was startled by his transformation from down-home friendly farmer earlier in the day to annoyed resident. "I didn't think I was snooping, Zed. The sisters didn't seem to want to share the owner's information. It's public record—I figured I could reach out to see if they were interested in cross-selling, seeing that they are a new business in town."

"Are we trying to involve every business in this?" Delilah asked from up front. It was odd she was not sitting next to Ava.

"Not necessarily," Mayor Nalini said calmly. "It

would be nice to include new businesses, but we can't force it on anyone."

"Businesses?" Zander hollered.

"Excuse me?" Mayor Nalini politely asked.

"What exactly do you mean by businesses? More are coming to the village?" Zed finished his brother's thought.

Delilah hastily grabbed her handmade colorful crossover bag from the front of the room and fumbled to get it around her as she stormed out, strands of long brown hair shaking loose from her bun.

I looked over at Ava with concern, but she just sat there staring straight ahead. What on earth was happening?

"There is land for sale, and there is a good chance some more businesses will be moving into our village. It will be good for the economy," the mayor said.

"Meaning it will be good to line your pockets," Mr. Seevers said through gritted teeth.

"Earl, no need to be like that," Bea said to her husband.

"It can help all of us," the mayor said as villagers began to whisper among each other.

"Does this have to do with Lou's murder?" Bradley asked.

"Yeah, why are you talking about money all of a sudden being good for all of us?" Ava piped up next to me. "Lou's murdered, the land's for sale, businesses moving in, and you're telling us it's best for all of us. Why is that?"

"And no one ever answered who Mr. Milano is," I whispered to Ava, hoping she would pick up that thread, since I didn't want to feel like I had to yell to be heard.

"Oh, right! Is this Mr. Milano fella the one with all the money moving businesses in here?" Ava bellowed.

Mayor Nalini did something he rarely ever has to do—he used the gavel to bring the meeting to order. "There are a lot of things up in the air right now. Let me address each issue that was just thrown at me one at a time," he said, looking to the crowd.

"First," he continued, "there is nothing concrete yet saying that businesses will move into the fields for sale. It is still in discussions. The village did put some money into the investment that Lou had going on—and lost it. Having businesses move into the fields would help with that."

Again, another uproar came up from the crowd. "I feel like you are being too generic; what do you mean 'the village' invested money—and who is in discussions?" Uncle Wylie asked.

"Everyone, everyone—listen—" The mayor hit his gavel again, but no one was listening.

A loud shrill rung through the air and everyone took a big breath in—I immediately shoved my fingers in my ears and moved away from Ava, who had her index finger and pinky in her mouth, whistling loudly to get attention.

"If you people want answers, then you need to be quiet and let the man talk!" she huffed.

"Thank you, Ava," the mayor said.

"Don't thank me, just tell us what's going on," she barked.

"I'm working with Mayor Cardinal in Tri-City. He would like to try and bring some businesses here so the people in the city can get a small-town feel."

"Cast Iron Creations is a restaurant—what we already have isn't enough for Mr. Big Shot Mayor Cardinal?" Ava made that sassy Latino head circular move: she meant business.

"I agree with you, Ava." The mayor looked down and took a deep breath. "Look everyone, I used some money to make an investment for adding more protection, like police for the village. I used Lou's investment and lost a lot of money. This is why I have been talking to the Tri-City mayor and thinking about his expansions."

"So, this is that urban sprawl Jolie was talking about," a Zimmerman brother bellowed moving angrily toward the Mayor up front. The other brother barreled up front too. Bradley and Meiser stepped in front of them.

"Gentlemen, there is no need to get in anyone's face. We are all having a discussion here," Meiser said.

The necks of the Zimmerman brothers were beet red and I swear I could see steam coming from their ears. They backed off and I noticed one took several deep breaths to work to calm down.

Mayor Nalini nervously fumbled with the gavel in front of him then took a breath while averting his gaze to glaring at me. I shrugged my shoulders. "Everyone needs to understand that urban sprawl is not illegal. Right now, nothing is definite. Let's adjourn this meeting for now and come back together next month when more is settled," the mayor said.

"What if you are out making decisions for all of us before next month?" Ava asked warily.

"I give you my word that won't happen," Mayor Nalini said.

His assistant, Abbey, spoke up. "I will back that up—I will call a meeting if anything comes up."

Everyone began to disperse—there was a lot of angry faces, shaking heads, and not-so-friendly hand gestures as the villagers hashed out everything that had just taken place.

Keith grabbed my elbow and pulled me aside, "Hey, do you have some time to talk? I have some information you might find interesting." His blond locks were always feathered back, and he always smelled of patchouli. I often wondered if I had made a mistake breaking things off with him.

"Sure, what's up?"

Meiser walked up behind me and said, "Hey, do you have a minute?" He turned to Keith and said, "Oh, I'm sorry, man—I didn't mean to interrupt."

Keith glared at Meiser. "No worries. I'll catch up with you later, Jolie." He stormed off.

That was awkward. These two weren't what I'd call friends, but Keith had never reacted in that way to Meiser before.

"Sorry about that, I didn't realize you two were having a private conversation," Meiser said, tilting his chiseled, strong jaw and scratching it. He had let his hair grow out a bit, and his naturally curly hair was tousled on top. It made me want to touch his hair.

"No problem, what's up?" I said again.

"You tell me—what was that envelope that had you so concerned before the meeting?"

I reached into my tote and pulled out the plastic bag with the envelope inside it and handed it over to him.

"That doesn't look good," he said grabbing the baggie. "I'm assuming I should take this to the station and have gloves on when I look at it?" His dark eyes clouded over with concern.

"That would be a good idea. I think it ties into that phone call I got in the middle of the night when Lou was murdered. Someone seems to think I'm snooping around too much."

"Well...are you?" he asked.

"No! I haven't done anything; I swear!" I said, using my index finger to cross over my heart in true Girl Scout style while crossing my fingers of my other hand behind my back.

"I'm having a hard time believing you. You have a way of being in the middle of all the drama," he said, grinning at me. "I'll check this out for prints and let you know what I find."

"Thanks," I said sullenly.

"So, we're on for the double date this weekend?" he asked.

"When?" This was news to me.

"Saturday evening at the new Italian restaurant. Ava made reservations for four. Didn't she tell you? What is going on with her lately?"

"Something is happening with her and Delilah, but she won't talk about it."

"Maybe we shouldn't go on this date. Doesn't seem like the best idea for a first date if the couple we are with is fighting," he said.

"It'll be fine. I'll get the details from her, and we'll meet you there," I said, throwing my tote over my shoulder to head out.

He grabbed my elbow as Keith had earlier. A

surge of excitement moved from my head to toes. "Yeah?" I turned around quickly, my shoulder-length blonde curls moving with me.

"I'll pick you up at your house, like a real date. Ava and Delilah can meet us there." He stared straight into my soul again.

All I could do was bob my head up and down in agreement. I had a feeling this was going to be some date.

Chapter Nine

I decided to get ready a little early on Saturday and pick Meiser up at his rental home. I knew where he lived but had never been inside before, and I wanted to see Stewart. Last fall, when Meiser bid on me at the Best Paws Auction for a date, he also adopted a cute one-eyed kitty—the only one that no one else had adopted.

I hoped he wouldn't mind that I was being unconventional in picking him up. I didn't grow up in a traditional family setting. My biological father made a trip on me psychologically, adding to my need to have walls to protect myself. My stepfather, Mike, was more of a *real* dad than the man who shared my blood. I had spent my late elementary years, middle school, and early high school years beginning to feel like a real kid again before he passed away from prostate cancer. That had destroyed me. This was right around the time Keith and I had been dating. I abruptly ended the relationship, not wanting to deal with it, and had closed myself off from relationships with men since then.

Meiser didn't know any of this baggage I carried

around, but I was hopeful he would go with the flow. I had given the traditional little life a try, and it had backfired on me—so here I go.

Since I was going to get my twenty-dollar spaghetti and meatballs tonight, it was an occasion to break out my little black dress with black silk pantyhose and red pumps. I wore my hair up in a loose bun with curls lightly framing my face. I swapped out my big tote for a smaller black purse. This was difficult for me. I wouldn't be able to carry my tablet and books for reading. I still had my phone with my reading app on it and my Bluetooth earbuds with my music app in case it got too loud. I could retreat internally by running to the restroom or out to the car for a bit. Hopefully, Meiser didn't mind how much of a handful I was.

I pulled up and parked in front of his rental home. It was a pale yellow-sided ranch with a small yard and a front porch with a swing and two rocking chairs on it. It looked like he had put new green shutters around the windows.

I clopped up the sidewalk in my heels and knocked loudly on the door. I heard a rustling sound by a bush toward the side of the house. I swore I saw what looked like a hooded figure jump out and run around the side. I took two steps back to try and see more, but I must have been imagining it. The blinds moved next to me and a one-eyed ragamuffin kitty peeked out at me. My mind must be playing tricks on me.

"Hi, Stewart!" I squealed, reaching my hand toward the cute cat. Stewart mouthed a meow and stretched a tiny little kitty paw back at me.

Meiser opened the door, looking confused. Then he bit his bottom lip and his already dark eyes stormed over even more as he looked me up and down before he grinned. "I thought I was the one picking you up tonight?" he asked, holding out his hand.

I wasn't sure what he was doing, but I took his hand. He spun me around to get a better look. I must admit I loved the attention.

"You look absolutely gorgeous," he said, pulling me into his house.

"Where's Stewart?" I said, avoiding his compliments before a red rash washed up my neck and cheeks. When I got nervous or embarrassed, I would get red blotches all over my arms, neck, and face. My choice in a V-neck and short-sleeved dress was not my best idea!

"Hey, Stew—kitty, kitty, kitty," he called.

I found myself drawn to this man, who typically was Mr. Tough, a straitlaced guy calling for his cat. Meiser was about ten years older than me, but he looked younger than his thirty-three years.

Stewart came strutting in, stretching his front paws on the carpet, then stretching both back legs behind him. He slowly moved toward Meiser to rub against his jeans. Stewart was a medium-haired white cat with patches of dark gray, tan, and black throughout his body. He had a long grayish-white tail. He was abused as a kitten and had lost his eye, which was now sewn shut, making him look like he was winking at you constantly.

Meiser picked him up and kissed him on his head. Stewart rubbed up against Meiser's goatee chin, purring loudly.

"Looks like you two are serious buddies," I said, rubbing Stewart's neck and reaching upward to kiss his head—this put me inches from Meiser's face, which turned to stare at me as we locked eyes.

He leaned in, and I reached up to rub my hand in his hair as we had our first kiss. His hair was as soft as it looked, and that messy curl feeling was nice except my ring got caught in some of his curls as the kiss intensified. Awkwardly, I left my hand in the same spot as not to jerk hair out of his head and continued to enjoy our lengthy kiss.

Stewart squirmed in his arms and I pulled back. "Hold on, my ring is caught on some of your curls," I said, reaching my other hand up to try and pull the curls off my ring as Stewart pushed hard against his chest, scratching him at the same time as my hand pulled back, taking out a small batch of curls before I could get the ring completely free.

"Ow," he yelped, reaching for his chest with one hand and his head with the other.

I couldn't help but giggle.

"Glad to know my pain amuses you," he said with laughter dancing in his dark brown eyes.

I continued to talk while laughing slightly. "It seems so perfect that our first kiss would involve a cat and some sort of awkward shenanigans."

"Yep, that seems to be the fate of our relationship—cats and shenanigans." He grinned, pulling me back to him.

"I can live with that." I looked up at his chiseled face—he had a long, pointy nose with a strong jaw and dimples when he smiled. It was a suggestive, sultry smile. "So, relationship?" I asked.

"I can live with that," he murmured as we continued to kiss—this time I willed myself not to run my hand through his hair.

As we untangled from each other, I looked at my watch and said, "You may want to get ready so that we can head over the restaurant. I'll play with

Stewart while you're getting dressed."

"Or we could opt out of the date and stay here," he said, reaching for me again.

"Hey, I'm not that kind of girl. Now go get ready, mister," I teased.

"Yes, ma'am," he said, saluting me and turning on his heels to head back to get dressed. I watched his backside as he moved toward his bedroom. Maybe I should have opted out of the date?

Meiser insisted on driving since I had shown up at his house. We pulled into the parking lot in his truck and, being a gentleman, he came around and got the truck door for me and held the door open as we walked inside. We were a little early and Ava and Delilah had not shown up yet, so we walked into the bar to have a drink.

I got a lemon drop martini while he opted for red wine. We were just settling in on our bar stools with our drinks when an adorable little brunette girl with long braids on each side of her head came running up to Meiser. She stopped short of pouncing on him, then calmly patted his leg with her hand.

"Gaze!" he exclaimed, hopping off the bar stool and picking the girl up in his arms with a big smile on his face.

She looked delighted to be in his arms. "Put me down, I'm not a baby," she said, giggling.

He plopped her back on the floor. "What are you doing here tonight?"

"The sitter couldn't get to our house in time, so Mom brought me with her," Gaze said. She looked down at the ground shyly, put her hands behind her back, and looked up at me.

"Gaze, this is my friend, Jolie," Meiser said.

I smiled at her and said, "I've never met a Gaze before. That is a beautiful name! I love your braids; did you do those yourself?"

Gaze shook her head hard back and forth, the braids slapping her chubby cheeks, and she giggled again.

Meiser put his hands on her shoulders to get her to stop.

"The sitter will be here shortly," Star said, sidling up next to Meiser and rubbing her hand on his forearm. "Are you picking up a to-go order, Mick?"

It threw me off to hear another woman call him Mick. I mostly called him Meiser and rarely called him Mick.

"Not tonight. Star, I'm on a date with Jolie, and we're meeting some friends here for dinner." He reached a hand back to me and smiled.

Mentally, I did a little two-step jig thrilled to have him call Ava and Delilah 'our' friends and to tell Star he was with me blatantly. Although she didn't seem too excited about it.

"I didn't know the two of you were dating!" Olive exclaimed as she walked up to our group with a big smile on her face. "That's so great!"

"Hi, Olive, how are you?" I asked.

"Doing pretty good. Business is booming tonight!"

"Yeah, I see that. I'm so happy Ava made a reservation," I said.

Olive looked back at Star in confusion, then at Meiser speculatively.

Ava and Delilah ambled up to our little group just then, holding hands. I was happy to see they had made up from whatever was going on between them before.

Gaze's eyes widened with excitement and this time she ran and attacked Delilah, yelling, "Miss Dewiwah!"

Delilah snickered and bent down to give Gaze a big hug. "There's my artist of the month!"

"What, no one told me you were an artist of the month," Star said, hands on hips.

"Not true, sis, we told you the other day when she came home," Olive said.

"You were sad that day, Auntie Star. You missed Grandma. It's okay," Gaze said.

"So is Gaze named after you?" Ava asked Star.

"Yep," Olive answered for her. "I was always jealous of Star's name, so when I had Gaze, I named her after my sis—like a stargazer."

"Very cool," Delilah said. "She is a wonderful artist in the making. We'll be having a show-and-tell for the family next Friday at the Dotting the Eyes showing. You both will have to come to see all of the amazing things she's done in our art class."

"Yeah, and all my stuff gets fancy frames since *I'm* the artist of the month," Gaze said in a singsong way, swaying her shoulders back and forth.

"Of course, we'll go to see, now let's get back to the kitchen. Jen will be here to pick you up soon, and we'll let them get to their table," Olive said as the trio moved back toward the kitchen. Gaze looked back at Meiser and gave him a smile and a wave, and he gave her a big grin and made a funny face at her, making her laugh.

I was enjoying seeing this side of Meiser.

"This place is pretty fancy. I want to see if they have any cast iron recipes on their menu," Ava said, browsing through the menu.

"Why?" I asked.

"Competition—you should be looking yourself," she huffed.

"Our business hasn't slowed down since they opened. We don't own all rights to cast iron cooking, you know. Plus, they do. Star told me the last time I stopped in."

"Since the snooty sister won't let us cross-sell, it sure seems that they view us as competition, so I'm going to see what kind of things they have on their menu." Ava gave me the stink eye, so I kept my mouth closed.

Delilah's body tightened slightly, and her lips thinned, but she remained quiet.

"I am trying the twenty-dollar spaghetti and meatballs. I heard that the sauce and meatballs are the owner's great-grandma's recipe from Naples. I've never heard of pasta costing so much, so I'm assuming it is delicious!" I exclaimed, then thought better of what I had just said. "Sorry, I must sound very cheap."

"Not at all, Jolie. It's a great thing when a person can take a moment to reflect on what they say and then find the courage to apologize," Delilah said, smiling at me and looking at Ava.

Uh-oh.

"You didn't sound cheap at all," Meiser said, trying to defuse whatever we saw building up between Delilah and Ava. "That is steep for pasta, and I agree with you that it must be fantastic. I'm going to get the same thing. Unless you'd like me to order something different so we can split our meals and try different things?"

He grinned so big his dimples were pulsating. I take it he could see from my expression that I thought his idea of splitting meals was a good one. Not only would Meiser have to put up with my baggage, but also my love of food. I know women are not supposed to eat a lot on a date, especially a first date, but I planned to get my money's worth from tonight. If he wanted to date me, then he needed to be prepared for my love of food.

"I would love to share my spaghetti and meatballs with you," I said.

"What else do you want to try?" he asked.

"Oh no, you choose what you want, and I'll be happy with anything you get," I said.

"I love Italian food. I want you to enjoy this night. You pick for us," he said leaning toward me and holding his menu so we could look at it together—even though I had my own menu, it allowed us to snuggle up to each other.

"Wow, what a gentleman!" Delilah said, looking at Ava again.

"I'm not a man," Ava barked, continuing to look over her menu.

"I didn't say anything," Delilah said.

"You've been insinuating that I'm not good enough for you for days now. I'm not a mind reader, Delilah. I've asked you numerous times to tell me what's going on and you refuse to do so. It doesn't give you the right to treat me like crap!" Ava threw the menu down.

Meiser and I exchanged an uncomfortable look. I went to speak up, but Ava cut me off.

"No need to play referee, Jolie. You've been

putting this date off for months now due to your fears of relationships. The last thing I want to do is ruin tonight for you," she said with tears in her eyes.

She stood up from the table and then looked down at Delilah. "When you are ready to tell me what is going on, then I'll be there for you. Until then, I'd suggest we stay away from each other," Ava said with a choppy voice, holding back sobs, and stormed out.

I reached over to grab Delilah's hand, but she pulled it back quickly. "What is going on, Delilah? You can talk to us," I said, looking at Meiser, who gave her a concerned look and nodded his head.

"I'm so sorry, you two. Ava was right; we shouldn't be ruining your date. I'll call an Uber and get out of your hair. I hope you two have a fabulous evening." She fumbled with her napkin, taking a quick drink of water and stomping off.

Meiser stood up and called after her, "I'm happy to run you home, Delilah."

That made my heart swell up.

Delilah didn't even look back at us but reached an arm straight back, shaking her hand in a wave while shaking her head no.

He sat back down and shifted uncomfortably in his seat.

The waitress came up to take our order just then.

"Do you want to stay?" Meiser asked me.

I took a moment to think about it. I wondered if I should go and check on Ava after all of that. I knew my friend well enough to know she would need to cool down for several hours before she'd be ready to see anyone, let alone talk to anyone. I shook my head. "I don't think we should put this date off any longer."

He gazed appreciatively at me. "Do you want another drink?"

"Sure," I said.

We placed our order, Meiser ordering the lasagna.

We were making idle chitchat when Mrs. Seevers walked up.

"Well, hello you two!"

My cheeks flushed. "Hi, Mrs. Seevers, are you here with your husband?"

"Lord no, child. We can't afford this place! Star was kind enough to give me a part-time job. I'm trying to help out with some of the money we recently lost."

Huh, I don't know why I had thought about the Zimmermans eating here but not about Mr. Seevers making reservations.

"Good for you, what are you doing here?" Meiser asked.

"Oh, I'm too old to be a waitress and carry all that food around. I'd dump it all over you! I'm the hostess and I answer phones. Speaking of food, looks like yours is here. I'll be getting back to work. Nice seeing you two. You look lovely together." She gave me a sly smile as she walked back to the front of the restaurant.

The food was indeed here, and it was a heaping mound of spaghetti and a huge chunk of lasagna. Each meal could have easily been split between two or three people. That alone made the cost seem more effective. The red sauce was the best sauce I'd ever had. I wished I could figure out who Mr.

Milano was, so I could try to cross-sell with him. Meiser had asked the waitress to have the cooks split the meals in half so we could share.

I was pleasantly surprised that he was like me. When it was time to eat, we ate—no chitchat.

Even though there was enough food there to feed four to six people, Meiser and I had no problem finishing it all off.

"Dessert?" the waitress asked, reaching to clear our empty plates.

I leaned back and put my hands on my stomach and groaned unattractively.

Meiser laughed. "Why don't you bring us the menu?"

I looked at him like he was crazy.

"We can take a look and order some to go," he said with a wink at me.

"Hmm . . ." I gave him a side glance with a skeptical look.

"There is no hidden agenda here. You made yourself perfectly clear earlier. You've wanted to try this place, and I want you to get the full experience. We'll order desserts and have them split them, and each of us can take them home for later," he said, reading my mind.

I grinned and nodded. "You know, I had serious doubts about you," I said.

"I know you did. Why's that?"

"It's a long boring story. But I'm finding I was wrong."

The waitress came back with the dessert menu. We looked it over and got an order of tiramisu and zeppoles to go—Meiser had them split them up again.

"One or two checks?" the waitress asked.

At the same time, I said, "Two" and Meiser said, "One," holding up his index finger.

She looked back and forth at us. "One, please," he said, reaching for his wallet and handing her a credit card.

She hurried away with his card.

"Why did you do that? I don't expect you to buy my meal. This is going to be really expensive!" I exclaimed.

"We're on a date. I want to buy," he said, taking my hand. "Now don't worry about it."

I looked down at my lap, scrunching my lips to one side.

"You always do that when you don't get what you want," he said.

"Do what?" I asked.

"You either get a really serious look and your lips get tight and thin, or you do what you just did and squeeze up your lips to one side of your face," he said, reaching up to brush his finger against my lips.

"Sorry, the fate of an only child," I said.

"Stop saying that. You have nothing to be sorry for."

"Why are you interested in me? You're older than I am, and you've worked your way into a position of detective. I'd think you'd want someone more mature and surer of who they are than me," I said.

"Does my age bother you?" he asked.

"It doesn't bother me at all—but it seems like my age should bother you."

"You don't think older men like to be with younger women?"

"Of course, they do. You are different, though. I'm not sure older men always want a lasting relationship with a younger woman, but you don't seem like you are *that* guy."

"You're right. I'm looking for a relationship with the right woman. You seem like the right woman." He shrugged his shoulders. "Why don't you tell me about this long boring story that is your life?"

The desserts came in to-go boxes to match the wooden décor of the restaurant, and was put in a beautiful maroon bag, and the waitress gave Meiser back his card. She also brought two cappuccinos.

"We didn't order these." I looked up at her with confusion.

"Olive asked me to bring them to you," she said, looking up front. Olive smiled and waved to us. We returned the smile and waved.

I traced the rim of my cup with my finger and looked down at the foaming drink and up at Meiser. "It's difficult for me to open up with anyone about stuff from my past."

"Me too," he said.

"It's nothing unusual. I grew up with a great family. My biological father was MIA most of the time. He and my mom divorced when I was young, and he didn't seem able to deal with it. He showed up when he felt like it and then would be gone for months or years at a time only to show back up out of nowhere and act like no time had passed." I drew back in my chair for distance.

"That's pretty rough for a young kid to understand," he said, rubbing my hand.

"My mom, grandma, uncle, and aunts were always there for me. My mom eventually married again, and my stepdad was incredible. I gave him all kinds of crap at first, though," I said, grinning as I thought of what a brat I was. "He wouldn't give up on me, though. He finally broke through my walls."

"Where's he at now?" Meiser asked.

"He passed away of prostate cancer when I was in high school. Before he died, I had finally started to feel normal. I started to trust again. I was even ready to date Keith, then all of a sudden Mike's— that's my stepdad's name—health turned, and it got worse over the course of a year, and he died." I felt a huge lump in my throat and worked to clear my throat to get ahold of my emotions.

"I'm so sorry," he said. "Thank you for sharing that with me. I know it wasn't easy."

"Thanks for listening. There's more to it all, but that's the gist of it. It's hard for me to trust men— for multiple reasons."

"I'm honored that you trust me," he said, taking the last few sips of his cappuccino.

I hadn't even started mine yet. I reached down to take a drink when he said, "I'm going to run to the restroom before we head out."

I nodded and took a big swig of my drink. As Meiser got up to head to the restroom, it seemed his legs gave out of him and he stumbled over, almost falling to the floor.

I hurried to sit my cup down. I held his arms as he grabbed the chair next to him and pulled himself up.

I looked at him full of concern.

"I must have sat too long, and my knees were

stiff," he said. Then he slowly limped to the restroom. I needed to ask him about all this stumbling I'd seen over the last several months.

When Meiser came back to the table, he grabbed the to-go bag and put an arm angled with his elbow out to help me up.

I waved to Mrs. Seevers but noticed she was holding her chest over her heart. Her face was ghost white.

"Call 9-1-1," I said to Meiser, moving toward her.

"Let's go sit. Lean on me," I said, moving her to the nearest seat.

Olive, who was at the bar and saw what was happening, brought some water.

"I feel flush. I'm sure it's nothing," Mrs. Seevers said. But I noticed she was sweating profusely.

The hospital was close by and the ambulance pulled up.

"No, child, please tell me that's not for me," she said, beginning to shake.

"Better to be safe," I said, calling Mr. Seevers. "I'll tell Earl to meet you there."

Meiser and I arrived at Bea's room to find Mr. Seevers sitting by her side.

"I can't believe you two called an ambulance! You could have just brought me here. I don't even want to think of how much this will all cost," Mrs. Seevers said, tears streaming down her cheeks.

"Now, Bea, your health is the most important thing. Don't go making the kids feel bad," Mr. Seevers said, holding her hand and squeezing it.

"What happened?" I asked, moving to the other

side of the bed, opposite of Mr. Seevers.

The curtain pulled back and Lydia stepped in. "Only family, I'm afraid you two will need to leave."

I glared at her.

"It's fine if they stay," Mrs. Seevers said, reaching for my hand. "I'm sorry I gave you a hard time, dear. I know you were looking out for me."

I squeezed her hand.

"The doctor will be in momentarily, but I wanted to let you know it's nothing too serious. It looks like you got some food poisoning," Lydia said.

"Food poisoning?" Meiser's voice shook. "Did you eat at the restaurant?"

"No, I told you it's too expensive."

"What's the last thing you ate?" I asked.

"Jolie, more than likely it's something she ate today, but if she's had multiple meals it will be hard to trace what it was," Lydia said as she narrowed her eyes at me.

"I'm not sure what all I've had today. I'm one of those people who eats small amounts of food all day long. The only thing I ate that Earl wouldn't eat was Jolie's Jalapeño Cheddar Cornbread. He doesn't do spicy foods."

The thought my food could do this made me speechless. I couldn't believe it was my food.

"Well, we will have you make a list of everything you can remember. If you think the two of you have eaten all the same things today, then we may want to keep you here to monitor too, Earl," Lydia said.

"You two go on. You were on a date. We'll be fine. Someday when you're our age, you'll understand how wonderful young love is and you won't want to ruin it for a nice young couple. So get,

get now!" Mrs. Seevers waved her hands at us.

"Okay, but call me tomorrow, please!"

We walked out to Meiser's truck in the hospital lot.

"Wow, what a wild date night," I said.

"Lots of action, but I think overall things worked out well for us," Meiser said.

"I told you some things about me. I must admit, I'm worried about you. Since I've met you, I've noticed you stumble a lot. Are you okay?" I asked nervously, turning the health topic to him. Last year, when I first met him, I remember him stumbling in the credit union—then again, our attempt at a Valentine's Day he seemed almost drunk at times.

"As you said earlier, it's a long story—and one that I do want to share with you," he said, briefly looking over at me with sad eyes. "But not tonight, if that's okay. It's not because I don't trust you. It's just that this was such a wonderful evening—mostly; let's keep it that way."

Now that statement did worry me, but I let it rest. We got back to his house, and he asked me if I'd like to come in, but I told him I was tired after the events of the night and asked him to kiss Stewart for me.

"I will be looking forward to your next visit when I'm holding Stewart and you are giving him a kiss," he said, eyebrows waggling.

I chuckled and shook my head back and forth. Then I leaned over to kiss him before heading to my car.

After I got home, fed the cats, cleaned out litter

boxes, and spent a little time loving on them, I got out of my uncomfortable clothes and changed into cutoff sweatpants and an oversized Tom Waits T-shirt. I grabbed my tablet to continue reading the newest Amanda Flower cozy mystery and was getting to a climactic part when the phone rang.

I jerked my head, glaring at the rude interruption, then looked at the clock. It was a little before eleven, which seemed late for a phone call. I hoped it was Ava, so I could see how she was doing.

"Hello," I said into the receiving end.

"Hey Jolie, it's Keith."

"Oh, hey, what's up?" I asked, reaching to rub my feet, which still ached from those stupid heels.

"Hey, yourself, sorry to call you so late. You know I wanted to talk to you yesterday at the meeting before the detective interrupted us," he said.

"Oh yeah, sorry about that. He didn't mean anything by it. We went out tonight, and he wanted to check on some things. What did you need?" I asked.

"You went out with him tonight?" He sounded hurt.

I hesitated, not knowing what tone to take or what to say next. I opted for a soft, "Uh—yeah."

"I guess I didn't know you were dating again."

"It's been six years, Keith. I will always appreciate that you were there for me when my dad, Mike, passed away," I said, meaning it.

"You're right. I suppose it's time. I guess I always hoped we could find our way back to each other," he said.

"I'm sorry, Keith, I don't see that happening." I

felt my gut wrench at the thought of hurting him again.

"I really think you need to be careful who you decide to date," he said with an air of protection in his voice.

"I truly like Mick," I said.

"I see. Well, I wish you well; take care, Jolie." He hung up.

Tears burned in the corner of my eyes as I wondered what his reasoning was for calling me.

Chapter Ten

"So, how'd it go last night? Do tell," Ava said, wiping down tables the next morning at our restaurant. Mirabelle's mom, Mary, was due to drop her and Spy off soon for a shift of a few hours.

"It was great. I like him," I said as she looked at me expectantly. "What? I like him a lot, okay?"

Ava grinned. "That's good to hear. Now, you weren't a slut, were you?"

"Nice." I rolled my eyes, heading back to the kitchen to get some cast iron monkey bread and a cast iron peach cake started. I wasn't planning on working an entire shift, but I wanted to bake a few things to help Carlos out. He'd been filling in for me when I couldn't work. Also, I wanted to see if he would be willing to take my morning shift the next day so I could meet with Mayor Cardinal.

I began multitasking, grabbing two of the skillets we used for baking and prepping them with some oil spray. Then I set ingredients aside by each assigned skillet, grabbing some mixing bowls and moving them near the Cuisinart mixer.

Ava had moved behind the counter and opened

the accordion blind we kept slid shut between the kitchen and the front of the restaurant when we were closed.

"What about you? Did you and Delilah get a chance to talk through things?" I asked, holding my breath.

"I Spy Slide," Ava said out of nowhere.

"Huh?" I gawked.

"The catchy name of our investigative tool. Isn't it perfect? I took some pictures of the land that is sectioned off around the Italian restaurant and added it to our slides. We'll need to update our information."

"Okay, sounds good. Why are you avoiding my question? What happened with Delilah?"

"I'm worried about her. She isn't acting like herself, but I meant what I told her. I'm done being her punching bag. She needs to come to me when she's ready to let me know what's going on," Ava said. "So, let's change the subject."

I began sifting some flour, adding baking powder, vanilla, and cinnamon to one bowl and grabbing another bowl for my wet ingredients.

"We need to add notes about Mrs. Seevers. Seems she got food poisoning last night. It could be innocent. It's weird hearing Lou could have been poisoned, then this happens to her," I said, watching Ava write it all down.

We were interrupted by a knock on the back door that led out to the alley and the dumpsters. Ava and I looked at each other and shrugged. I walked to the door. "Hello, who's out there?" I called cautiously. Ava had walked back behind me and grabbed a rolling pin.

"Who do you think would be knocking from the back?" Aunt Fern yelled.

I pushed the door open to find not only my aunt, but Uncle Wylie, Mom, and Grandma Opal, all coming through the door in a line.

"Now just what do you think you were going to do with that?" Grandma Opal bent her head as her glasses fell on her nose. She looked at Ava with amusement and pointed to the rolling pin. "You baking today?"

"Naw, if anyone was up to no good, I was going to handle it," Ava said, taking the pin and slapping it in her other hand threateningly. Flour flew up in her face and she coughed.

Laughter erupted from my family. "What are you going to do, flatten 'em out like a pancake?" Uncle Wylie asked. More mirth.

"I'll show you what I was going to do," Ava said, coming up on Uncle Wylie. Those two had a history of having wrestling matches since she was a kid. He liked that she was a tomboy and used to play basketball with her and have her lifting weights with him.

He playfully grabbed the other end of the rolling pin, and a tug of war began to take place in the kitchen.

"Guys knock it off—you are going to break something," I said. Meanwhile, the rest of my family egged them on.

Mary, Mirabelle's mom, had a key to the front and had come in with Mirabelle and Spy. With all the chatter in the kitchen, no one had heard them.

"WOOF!" Spy let out a loud bark.

We all stopped in our tracks.

"Sorry, I knocked, but no one heard us, so I used the key you gave us," Mary said quietly.

I reached over and grabbed the rolling pin from the two goofballs. I turned to Mary and said, "Sorry about that; these two were messing around." Then I turned to Mirabelle. "Hello, beautiful, how are you today?" I reached into the cabinet over the fridge to grab Spy a treat. He stayed sitting but wagged his tail on the ground, looking up as I fed it to him.

"We're doing great. It's a really pretty day out today," Mirabelle said.

I loved how she always answered with "we," meaning her and Spy.

"Mirabelle and Spy have an art class with Delilah in an hour, but she wanted to know if she could work an hour here first, then I'll pick her up and take her over there," Mary said.

"I can take her if you don't mind," I said. "I am going to finish prepping a couple of things to bake here, then I was heading out. I don't mind at all."

"That would be great. Is that okay with you, Mirabelle?" Mary asked.

"Oh yeah. Miss Jolie, can we go on your bike?" she asked.

"I don't have it today," I said, wishing I would have brought it now.

"We're not doing anything right now. We'll drive over to your house, and your mom can ride it over, then we'll follow you over. I haven't seen Delilah in a while," my grandma said.

"That'd be great," I said. "Wait, why are you all here?"

"We were all heading to the mall and thought we'd stop in to say hi. We're having lunch together later," Mom said.

"Okay," I said, tapping my fingers loudly on the counter. This is what I meant when I told Ava that, sometimes, I wished my family had moved. I love them, but I felt like my entire life was devoured by them. I felt like I couldn't breathe at times.

Mary gave Mirabelle a big hug and kiss and gave Spy a rub on his head and turned to leave. She turned back as she got to the door. "I can pick her up after her lesson this afternoon."

"Sound's good, Mary. I'll let Delilah know," I said.

Once Carlos arrived at the restaurant, I filled him in on what I had prepped for the day and let him know if he had time, I'd like him to make an extra peach cake for Betsy to sell at her shop.

Meanwhile, my mom and my family went to pick up my bike and were back. We all got ready to head to Delilah's shop, Crafty's Corner. Delilah not only owned Crafty's Corner, but also ran the Nuu Art Gallery two doors down.

My bike was now a two-seater, and we had put a side seat on it. Mirabelle loved my last bike, which I called Gertrude—Mirabelle calls this bike Gertrude Jr. It wasn't safe for her to ride on my last bike and she isn't able to ride a bike. So I had gotten a two-seater to ride her around town. But then Spy looked so sad, watching his Mirabelle leave him, that Uncle Wylie helped me find a way to attach a small sidecar that allowed Spy to ride with us. It was one of my favorite things to do.

Aunt Fern, always the dog lover, wanted to help get Spy into his seat. She gave him a couple of treats for the ride.

"I already gave him a treat earlier today," I said. "Don't forget that Mary said we couldn't fatten him up too much."

"He's a good boy and, besides, these are those healthy treats—he deserves something for being such a great host!" Aunt Fern exclaimed.

I gave up and helped Mirabelle put her helmet on as Aunt Fern finished getting Spy situated. He seemed to be smiling up at her.

We took our time. I even looped around to the center of the village and then doubled back to the art studio so we could have more time to sightsee. Mirabelle was so observant of the little things and would "ooh" and "ahh" at her surroundings, pointing out pretty flowers and how big trees were. Her vision was altered, but she still found the beauty in all things. The rest of my family took advantage of the nice weather and walked across the alleyway to meet us there. They were waiting, since I had done a few loops around town.

We got to Crafty's Corner, and I helped Mirabelle off my bike while Aunt Fern took care of Spy.

I was hoping I'd get a chance to talk to Delilah privately and see if I could figure out what was going on with her.

When we walked in, Delilah was working with Gaze, making a silly-faced small flowerpot. Delilah smiled up at me, but I noticed she also had an uncomfortable look.

"Wow, that looks very cool! Will you be selling these?" I asked, looking down at Gaze and smiling.

She looked up at me but didn't seem to recognize me, as she was too involved in painting black glasses on her silly face.

"I doubt Gaze will want to sell this. She mentioned wanting to give it to her Aunt Star to help cheer her up," Delilah said, standing up from the floor.

I noticed my family had taken Mirabelle to her cubby at the back of the shop so Mirabelle could show them some projects she had been working on. Other kids were working on different projects, while volunteers moved around the room to help out and support their creativity. Delilah did a lot with the village kids during summer months when they weren't in school, and parents appreciated having a safe and fun place to leave their kids for a few hours daily. Ava and I had volunteered to read to the kids some days and to help the older kids with cooking and baking too.

Delilah moved me into her tiny office space, which had enough room for a small table and a filing cabinet. I stood in the doorway. "When I met Gaze last night, she mentioned something about Star being sad last week," I said.

"Yeah, Olive and Star have had a rough year. Their mom had a stroke at a young age, and it affected her movement and speech. She had to be put in a nursing home and passed away last year," Delilah said, rubbing her head.

"I had no idea. Wow, that's got to be difficult losing your mom at such a young age!"

I noticed out of the corner of my eye that my family had moved to a table nearby to sit with Mirabelle as she worked on a project.

"I wanted to ask you—" I started to ask when a man I didn't recognize walked up behind me.

"Excuse me, I'm sorry to interrupt, but is Delilah here?" he asked.

"Oh hi, Mr. Nestle," Delilah said furtively, getting up to move past me.

"Sorry, I'm going to head over and see what my family is up to," I said, taking a cue that this was private.

My uncle, aunt, mom, and grandma had paper plates, glue, scissors, construction paper, and markers out and my Aunt Fern was looking something up on her phone.

"What are you all working on?" I asked.

"We are going to make a Spy face!" Mirabelle squeaked in glee.

"A Spy face?" I asked.

"I'm looking up directions on how Mirabelle can make a picture of Spy with these materials," Aunt Fern said. "Let's grab this yellowish felt and draw some shapes that look like Spy's ears first then cut them out to put on top the plate. Then we'll make his cheeks and work from there."

"Oh, I see—the plate is the face, and you'll add the ears and cheeks! Neat!" I exclaimed.

I looked over and could tell that Delilah was not happy. Her body sagged over, and she looked extremely stressed out. Mr. Nestle was shaking his finger at Delilah. For a moment, I was tempted to go back over to see if she needed help, but he stormed out of the shop, slamming the door and making all of us jump.

Everyone's eyes went to Delilah, who looked like she was ready to cry, but she said, "Sorry about that; it must be windy outside." With that, she went to her tiny office and shut her door.

Delilah never came back out of her office before we

left. I rode back to the restaurant to check in on Ava.

"Hey, how's business going?" I asked, sitting up at the counter.

"Great, we got swamped right after you left, but it just slowed down," Ava said. This was the standard comment. Every time I left, and Ava was there, she was inundated with customers, and it always seemed to slow down whenever I got back.

I heard our door jingle and turned on my stool to see Mrs. Seevers come in, all dressed up.

"Well, look at you! You look spiffy," Ava said.

"Thank you; I'm happy to hear you have a sense of a well-dressed lady and what she can bring to the table," Mrs. Seevers said.

"Feeling better, I take it?" I asked.

"You know it! We never figured out what caused the food poisoning, so Earl and I threw a bunch of stuff out to be safe. He never got sick, though." She made the spitting *to to to* sound three times on her index and middle finger to signal warning off bad things.

"Well, I'm happy you are feeling better so quickly," I said.

"I don't think it was anything too serious. I'm an old lady, but I don't let too much keep me down—that's why I'm here today!"

Ava and I looked at each other speculatively.

"I'm here to ask you, kind ladies, if I can fill out an application," Mrs. Seevers said.

"Fill out an application?" I repeated.

"Well, yes, I think I could add a lot to this quaint little restaurant of yours," she said.

"I'm sure you could, but what about the job at M&M's restaurant? You were retired for quite some time. Are you sure you can handle two jobs?" I asked.

I realized as soon as the words left my mouth that I should have kept my mouth shut. Mrs. Seevers' cheeks burned red, and she looked down and fiddled with the clasp on her purse.

Thankfully, Ava noticed I had put my foot in it again and piped up with, "You know, we have some applications in the back office. Are you looking for full or part-time?"

Mrs. Seevers smiled appreciatively. "Oh, I'm only looking for a few hours a week. Just want to make a little more for running-around money."

"Of course, let me go back and grab those," I said, taking an opportunity to remove myself from the situation.

I was looking through the desk drawer, trying to find our standard application, when Ava jumped in the room. "What is going on? Can you believe it? Do we need any help right now?"

I shot up out of the chair at her brisk entrance. "You scared me!"

"Sorry, I didn't know what else to say to her after you made it all awkward."

"I didn't do it on purpose. She surprised me!"

"Me too, but you didn't see me putting my foot in my mouth," Ava said.

"Where are the applications? We just had them not too long ago when we hired Magda," I said, sitting back down and frantically pushing papers around in the drawer.

"I put them up front under the counter," Ava

said.

"You what?"

"It seemed smart to keep them up front in case people came in asking for an application," she said.

"Mmm hmmm—you are right. That does make sense. So, why did you send me back here, leaving Mrs. Seevers out there all alone? Now, what are we supposed to do?" I panicked.

"I don't know; I freaked out when you made it weird. I can't take care of everything," she said, hands on hips.

"Uh, come on, we can't leave her up there any longer—it's just going to get weirder," I said.

I pushed through our swinging doors and stopped suddenly when I saw Meiser talking to Mrs. Seevers. Ava rammed right into my back, and I flew forward into the counter.

"There you two are, I was beginning to get worried," Mrs. Seevers said.

"Uh yeah, Jolie forgot that when we hired Magda, we moved the applications up here. Sorry about that," Ava said.

I glared at Ava as Meiser moved toward me to check on me.

"Here they are," Ava said, handing one over to Mrs. Seevers, who pulled a pen out of her purse.

"Your beau here was just telling me all about your first date the other night," Mrs. Seevers said, giving Meiser and me a suggestive look. "I'm so happy all my nonsense didn't ruin it."

I felt blotches going up my neck and moving to my face, "Of course not! I'm happy we were there."

"I'm hoping our insurance will cover most of the expenses," Mrs. Seevers said, continuing to fill out her application. "Earl told me he talked to you last week, Jolie. I know you realize why I need to work now."

"I'm sorry, Mrs. Seevers. I was—"

She interrupted me. "It's okay, child, no one ever can get too settled in this life of ours. Things are always happening to alter our paths."

"I Spy Slides," Ava blurted out.

Mrs. Seevers and I stared slack-jawed at Ava.

"I'm sorry, dear, I don't think I understand," Mrs. Seevers said.

"Oh, it's a goofy game Jolie and I play. It would take too long to explain, but you mentioned *altered paths*." Ava's chin moved down as she drug out those words, looking at me. "And I was just thinking we could add that to our game."

"Good one," I said. I had no good comeback.

Thankfully, Carlos walked in and noticed the application. "Mrs. Seevers, you will be coming to work here?"

Mrs. Seevers smiled at Carlos. "I'm not sure if I've got the job yet."

"Ava and I will need to see if we need the help right now. But we will definitely call Mrs. Seevers back for an interview to see if there is anything we can do to help," I said.

"Now, I don't want your charity, girls. If you don't need the help, then you don't need the help— no sense in spending money you don't need to spend. You're a newer business, and you need to keep your finances straight. Don't I know it," she said.

"Yeah, but we can always use some people here to help us out during certain busy times. Let us talk about it and look into it. I promise we'll tell you the truth if we can't do anything," I said.

Mrs. Seevers looked at Carlos and said, "Now don't you worry, dear. Even if I don't get the job, I'll still be in here all the time for the delicious food, and I'll get to visit with everyone."

Mrs. Seevers slid her application across the counter and walked out.

Meiser asked me, "Does Mirabelle only like dogs or does she like cats too?"

"She loves all animals," Ava interrupted enthusiastically. Ava loved any conversation that included Mirabelle.

I laughed, "Mirabelle is great with my cats."

"Well, I was thinking maybe you could bring her and Spy over for a visit with Stewart," Meiser said.

"Of course, I can," I said. "Do you think Spy and Stewart will get along?"

Ava spoke up, "Oh, I'm sure Spy is great with cats. He's trained and all."

I looked at Meiser. "How will Stewart do with Spy?"

"They'll be fine. Dr. Libby was going to use him as an office cat because he got along with all kinds of animals before I adopted him," Meiser said, referring to our village veterinarian.

"I'll call her mom, and we'll try to set it up for this week; I promise."

Things were slowing down. Carlos and Magda were taking care of the business, so Ava and I went back to the office and shut the door.

I pulled up the I Spy Slides. "Please don't do that again."

"Do what?"

"Blurt out 'I Spy Slides' out of the blue!"

"Why do we have a secret name for it if we can't use it?"

I hated when she made a good point.

"Maybe try to ease it into conversation a little better if we ever need to use it again."

"Ten-four, Captain." Ava saluted me.

I rolled my eyes. "Okay, why the land pictures again? There are no notes here."

"It's weird. All of a sudden land going up for sale that people lost to Lou, who is dead. I don't know what to write down, but don't you think they are connected?"

"Good point." I wrote notes under the collage of pictures of the land:

- *Zimmerman's land being sectioned off*
- *Rumors of urban sprawl*
- *Mayor Nalini not telling townspeople the entire truth?*
- *Corruption? Legal? Illegal?*
- *Milano—owner of M&M's Italian restaurant*

"I'm going to add something under the Seevers' slide about her food poisoning. I wish we knew the source of it."

"I think you need to add a note about how irate the Zimmerman brothers acted at the meeting. They looked ready to pummel someone," Ava said.

"Should I add that by their pictures or on the slide with the land or both places?"

"You are so obsessive compulsive. Move their picture and notes over with the pictures I took of their land. I swear, what would you do without me?"

"Be saner," I mumbled under my breath while doing what she said.

"I heard that!"

"Hmmm?" I said. "Hey, what's that glint in the field?"

"What are you talking about now?" Ava asked.

I clicked on a picture and enlarged it. Ava and I both leaned our faces right up to the screen.

"It's got something blue in it, I think," Ava said.

I enlarged it a bit more but couldn't see any better.

"Do you have the original picture on your phone?"

Ava reached in her back pocket and scrolled through her pictures. She pulled it up, zooming in.

"It looks like blue liquid in a small vial," I said.

Ava and I looked at each other quizzically.

Chapter Eleven

It was Monday morning and I had a little time to kill before heading to Tri-City to meet the mayor. I was sitting out back on my cushy swing enjoying looking at my garden and sipping on some tea. I was debating telling the mayor how rude it is to have his assistant schedule an appointment without giving a specific reason, but I knew I'd chicken out when the time came.

I'd seen Mayor Cardinal on TV before and felt he carried a staunch appearance. He had slicked-back strawberry-blonde hair and freckles, giving him a guy-next-door look. Then you looked at his suits, and he had a piercing look that made me feel nervous. I didn't trust him. I could see why people voted for him, but I wouldn't have done so.

I was lost in thought when I heard scratching at the screen door and looked to see Lenny, D.J., and Bobbi Jo standing at the door looking at me. Bobbi was the one scratching the screen up. Sam Jr. had to be hiding under a bed somewhere. This caused me to look at my watch and made me realize it was time to head out to make my appointment on time.

"Okay, little ones, back up," I said, putting my foot at the door to make sure no one snuck out on me. My three cats happily turned around and moved toward the living room. D.J. jumped in the cat bed that I had positioned by one window where the sun shone in on her, while Lenny and Bobbi jumped up on the cat tree that I kept right in front of the picture window. Their cat tree had five layers with a circular enclosure and a triangle layer, and one layer had tile, and the top was carpet. Bobbi Jo, being the boss of the house, took the top layer while Lenny laid in the triangular section soaking in some sun. I guess they didn't want out, after all, just wanted mom to come in.

I headed out the door to my car as Meiser was pulling into the drive.

"Headed to work?" he asked, getting out of his truck.

"Nope, I'm heading to the city. I have a meeting with the mayor," I said, knowing this would catch him off guard.

"What?"

"I don't know. His assistant called me last week and set up an appointment for this morning. I have to head out now," I said, pecking him on the cheek.

"Do you know how long the meeting will be?" he asked.

"No idea, but I'm assuming not long. I can't imagine why he needs to speak to someone like me," I said.

"Well, I can't imagine why he hasn't contacted you by now! All important men should need to speak with someone like you," he said, grabbing me around the waist.

I crooked my head upwards in confusion. "I

believe you were going for a compliment there, but I'm not quite sure how to take it."

He laughed with me.

"Okay, I'll let you go. Want to bring Mirabelle over tonight after work to visit Stewart?"

"You really want her to meet your cat, don't you?" I asked.

"Sure, but I'm looking for any excuse to see you too," he said, bending down for a kiss.

He pulled back to leave and gave me that sultry smile and there were those dimples. I was definitely doomed!

I arrived a little early to my meeting and took the opportunity to hit the ladies' room to freshen up a bit after the ride into the city—not to mention my morning tea was pushing through me.

I was getting ready to come out of the stall when I heard two women arguing. I decided to stay put for fear of awkwardness.

"No way, Mr. Nestle told me that the deal was all but cinched with purchasing the art district. He met with the lady who runs the craft store yesterday." This lady had a high-pitched nasally voice.

"I don't think she's going to budge. That's why the mayor wants to step in and see what he can do," said a deeper raspy voice. I assumed this lady was a smoker based on how much she kept coughing and clearing her throat.

"You can't light up in here," the nasal lady said.

I knew she was a smoker!

"I don't have time to go outside, Pam, please just give me a break," a raspy voice said.

"Oh, go ahead, Tonya," Pam said.

I could smell the sweetness of the nicotine wafting in the stall. Tonya, she was the woman who called to set up my meeting.

"John has someone coming in to meet him this morning. She should be here soon," Tonya said while exhaling her smoke.

"Maybe he can talk some sense into the country bumpkins," Pam said.

Was I the country bumpkin?

"Whatever, if he wants it to get done, then he'll do what is necessary to get it done," Tonya said, turning on the faucet. I could see through the crack in the stall that she was putting her cigarette under the water before throwing it away. I could tell Tonya had extremely tight curls, and they were sticking way out of her head like wires.

"I guess you'd know, wouldn't you, mistress," Pam said with a sarcastic tone, hanging on the word *mistress.*

The women left, and I took that as my cue to exit and get to the office. I hung back to wash my hands and fix my hair and straighten out the blazer I brought with me, making sure the women were long gone in case they were referring to the mayor and myself.

I walked out and looked at the black billboard on the wall by the elevator that told me where the mayor's office was located. I was on the right floor, but it was at the back of the building.

I headed around the corner, moving past cubicles, then down a long hallway of offices until it gave way to a large round waiting room with no one in it and a large mahogany desk where Tonya sat.

"Hello, are you Jolie?"

"Yes, ma'am," I said, rubbing my hands on my tan trousers and pulling my navy blazer down. I always fidgeted when I was nervous.

"Have a seat, please," she said.

I sat down, looking up at a high ceiling. Gorgeous artwork made circular swirls of colors that complemented each other around the entire circle of the ceiling.

The mayor walked out of his office and bent down to give Tonya a piece of paper. She looked up at him and grinned big. I noticed he placed his left hand, with a wedding ring on it, on her shoulder. He squeezed it and winked at her.

"Well, this must be Jolie Tucker, the co-owner of that delicious Cast Iron Creations restaurant in Leavensport, Ohio," he said, making a point to walk around the desk and come to me. He had a huge painted-on smile and gave me a firm handshake.

I was happy that even though it was warm outside I had opted for a blazer. I could feel the rash moving up my arms.

"Hello, sir, it's a pleasure to meet you," I said quietly. I noticed out of the corner of my eye that Tonya was watching our encounter and seemed satisfied I had shown the proper respect to her boss.

"Come on into my office," he said in a booming voice. He grabbed Tonya's shoulder again as he walked by and said, "Hold all my calls while I'm in this important meeting, dear."

"Sure thing, Mr. Mayor." Tonya attempted a flirtatious voice, but it came out crass.

The mayor pushed a bowl of cookies and candy across his desk to me. "Take some, Jolie. I'm sure this is nowhere near as good as your cooking, but I have a sweet tooth and have to keep sugary goods with me all the time. It's a bad habit to have."

"No, thank you, sir. I had breakfast before I drove here today."

"Sorry about having to have you drive to me, Jolie. Hopefully, one day it won't take so long to get from your village to the city," he said, taking a hard candy and unwrapping it and popping it into his mouth, then smiling big at me again.

"Oh, why is that, sir?"

"Well, that's part of the reason for this meeting today. Many people in the city are charmed by your little village, and we've found in running some reports that some of the businesses in your village make a lot more money than some of the best places our city has to offer," he said, leaning back in his chair and linking fingers on his firm stomach. For a man who loved sugar, he looked to be in top shape. "One of those places is your restaurant. In fact, that entire art district by you does amazing business compared to many of our galleries. Your little cast iron restaurant puts out some wonderful food!"

"Have you been to our restaurant, sir?" I couldn't help but ask after he had made so many references to how good our food was.

He sat up straight and coughed. "Well, I haven't had the pleasure to dine there, but I've heard from friends that your food is fabulous."

Now I trusted him even less.

"So, what is the reason for the meeting?" I asked.

"Wanting to get right to the point; I can appreciate that in a lady," he said, switching to all business. "Jolie, we are looking to expand and move some of our restaurants and galleries into your village. One of my associates, Mr. Nestle, is looking to purchase some of the buildings in your village to save the cost of having to rebuild. I'm sure you've seen the land for sale by the highway leading to the city. I'm anticipating we'll make enough money to be able to get buses that go from the city to the village and back multiple times a day." He beamed.

This was very overwhelming for me to hear. Everything I'd heard about this in the village had been negative to date—which affected my initial reaction to all this.

"I'm still not sure where I come in with all of this," I said.

"Before I dive into anything, I want take it upon myself to get to know who I will be working with. Now, I happen to know that your co-owner Ava is dating Delilah Samson. My understanding is a meeting with you would be much more civil than a meeting with Miss Martinez."

I felt my face heat up. That was a slam on Ava.

"We are having a difficult time getting Miss Samson to cooperate in selling one of the buildings. Plus, we know her parents own the other two buildings, and they are run by her and will eventually go to her. I was hoping that you'd be willing to work with me on this. I can promise you I will make it worth your time and effort—that business of yours is already booming. I can guarantee what you make will triple within six months," he said, face altering to that resembling a weasel.

Anger surged through me. I wasn't quite sure of all the reasons I was angry, but I knew his comment about Ava being uncivil and Delilah not cooperating really upset me. "So, based on everything you just said, I think that you think I am an idiot," I said, calmly standing and crossing my arms. Even in anger, I tended to be eerily calm, except with my family—and Ava.

The mayor's face turned into pure innocence. "Why, Miss Tucker, whatever would make you think that? I think the exact opposite of you, or you would not be sitting in here right now."

I smiled sweetly. "You're good—a little too good," I said, then turned to head to the door.

"This meeting is not over, young lady." The sweet, innocent voice was gone and replaced with one of anger and scolding.

"With all due respect, Mayor, you have wasted enough of my time. Best of luck with your plans moving forward," I said and stormed out.

Chapter Twelve

I came into Cast Iron Creations hot. I jerked my blazer off and slammed it on the counter with my tote. Ava was taking an order but looked up at me concerned.

She walked around the counter and put the order into Carlos, who had been kind enough to work my shift while I wasted his and my time at that stupid meeting.

"Carlos, thanks so much for coming in on your day off. I will work one of your shifts this week. May I please ask another favor—can you stay a little longer so I can talk to Ava?" I asked.

"This is no problem for me. Would you mind not picking up another shift so I can make more this week?" he asked.

"Of course, Carlos! Thank you so much; I appreciate it."

"Thank you," he said, then grabbed the ticket Ava had. "I'll take care of this right now."

"Why are you acting like a nut job?" Ava grabbed my arm and pulled me off to the side. "You are frightening the customers and Carlos."

I rolled my eyes, thinking that she frightens everyone *way* more than I ever could.

"I don't even know where to start. So much is running through my head right now. I can't sort through it," I said, starting to hyperventilate slightly. I get overwhelmed more easily than most people. I'm somewhat of a high-maintenance friend at times in my own way.

"Girl chillax—come back to the kitchen and get some tea to calm yourself," she said, walking me back to the kitchen.

I smiled at Carlos and poured some hot water into a cup. I put a chamomile teabag in it with honey and milk and we went back to the office.

I took a few sips, then said, "Oh crap, hold on—I need to call Mary to see if I can take Mirabelle and Spy over to Meiser's house tonight. I will forget if I don't do it now."

Ava's eyes widened and she kept her head perfectly still while moving her pupils to the side to look at me like I'd lost it, "K," she said, "I'm going to go out and check on Magda and everyone while you do this, then I'm coming back so you can tell me what is up."

I shook my head and looked up Mary's number in my phone and called to get permission to take Mirabelle and Spy for a visit to Stewart tonight.

"That would be wonderful, Jolie. I haven't had a night out in so long—what time do you think you'd bring her home? Also, will you make sure she gets dinner—oh, and Spy. I should drop off some food for him too."

Mary was truly a superhero in my eyes. Taking care of Mirabelle and Spy as a single mom and working full-time was rough on her. She loved her daughter dearly, but she would be her caregiver for life.

"Mary, just tell me what Spy needs and I'll take care of it. Also, I have a guest room if you'd like Mirabelle to stay the night, so you can get some rest or go do whatever you want," I offered.

"Oh no, I wouldn't be able to get rest if she wasn't with me. I'm sorry if that is offensive. You know I trust you. It's just—"

I interrupted her. "I know how much you love her. It was just an offer, and there are no hard feelings. That offer always stands too in the future, so that you know."

"You truly are a gift, Jolie!" Mary exclaimed.

"Well, you know how much we all love Mirabelle and Spy. Let's see—I should have her home by nine. Is that okay?"

"Sounds great; see you then."

I drank more tea, took a deep breath, and headed out to see how things were going.

Ava was taking food to a table, and it looked as if the lunch crowd was thinning out. "My mind is spinning. It's like ever since Lou was murdered, the village has been in complete chaos. But it hasn't. Does that even make sense?" I asked.

"No, what happened at that meeting?" Ava asked.

"Well, the first thing you need to know is that I know what is going on with Delilah and it's not you," I said.

"What? Is she okay?"

"I don't know—there is a man who has been pressuring her to sell the property she owns and her parents' property. He wants to buy the art district. I saw him there when I went with my family, and she looked upset, but I didn't know what it was about until I met with Mayor Cardinal today."

"Who is it? He's going to be sorry!" Ava slammed a fist on the counter.

"Now who's making a scene?"

"Sorry," she said, taking a breath. "Why wouldn't she tell me?"

"Probably pride." I shrugged my shoulders.

"What is going on in this village?" Ava asked, rubbing her forehead.

"That's just what I mean. Things have been looming—rumors about urban sprawl since last fall. Ellie murdered last year, now Lou. Financial fraud and it's all supposedly Lou's fault. Now more land is up for sale, and Mrs. Seevers is looking for a second job? I'm getting weird phone calls and notes. Delilah's being threatened by this Mr. Nestle, who may be connected to Mayor Cardinal, who wants to buy out the art district here in town—"

I was interrupted by Bradley and Lydia, who had just walked in. "Did you say Nestle?" Bradley asked.

"Yeah," Ava said, "he's been sniffing around messing with your sister—did you know that or are you still too busy to talk to her?"

"I didn't know that, but what I do know is that this Nestle guy is the one who was working with Lou," Bradley said through gritted teeth.

"Maybe he had something to do with Lou's murder," I said. "I have a hard time believing that Lou would do this to people. Maybe this guy blackmailed Lou, and then Lou decided to come clean, and then Nestle killed him?"

"I'm just happy you aren't blaming me this

time," Lydia snapped.

Okay, so another sore spot was that Lydia and I were somewhat frenemies. Last fall, I thought she was involved in Ellie's murder—we already had issues that dated way back and that did not help our situation.

"Nope, not you—*this time*," I said with a grin. She didn't look amused.

We were all chatting at the counter as Star came in and sat at the opposite end of the counter.

"Hi, Star," I said. "You are welcome to join us."

"Hey, folks, no that's okay I'm going to look over the menu and place an order to go—I brought my laptop to get a little work done while I wait." She smiled and pointed to her small two-in-one with her.

"We heard about what happened with the weird note and phone calls, Jolie," Bradley said.

Lydia put her hands up in innocence, and I cut her off before she could say it. "I know, it wasn't you," I said.

She grinned.

"Yeah, it was weird because the letter had cut-out letters like from a magazine. What was even stranger is we saw some projects like that hung up over at Crafty's Corner the other day," I said.

Star's food had just come out, and she walked over to the group, "Hey, Jolie—sorry to interrupt," she said and looked to the group. "Before I leave, I wanted to tell you that Olive and I discussed it and we are interested in cross-selling with you. Give me a call sometime, and we can set up a meeting." She handed me a business card.

"Will do," I said, smiling as she waved. I turned

around to see Ava standing and glaring at me. "What?"

"You don't think Delilah has anything to do with your letter, do you?"

"Of course not. I saw it at Crafty's Corner when Nestle was there," I said.

"I have to call Delilah and let her know I know what's going on," Ava said.

Bradley said, "Ava, do you mind if we walk over together to check on her?"

Ava looked beside herself. "I think she would love that."

Nothing like tribulation to bring the family together.

I pulled up to Meiser's place with Mirabelle and Spy in tow. Meiser must have been watching for us because he came strutting out in jeans, fitted T-shirt, and tennis shoes. He looked just as amazing dressed down as when he had his shirt and tie on.

"I told Stewart he better get his nap in early today because he had some company coming tonight." Meiser beamed at Mirabelle as he opened the car door for her.

I noticed her face flushed and she smiled up at him. "Spy and I are excited to meet Stewart."

I got Spy from the back seat and walked him over to Mirabelle. She took his lead, and we all trotted up to the front door.

I looked up at Meiser with a nervous look—cats and dogs don't always get along. He gave me a reassuring look, and we let Mirabelle and Spy go in first and came up behind them.

"What's that noise?" Mirabelle asked.

"I put Stewart in a room so I could go get him once you all got in here and got situated," Meiser said.

"Oh, well, let's sit Spy so Stewart can come out," Mirabelle said excitedly.

Spy took that as a command to sit and sat right there by the door.

"No, silly, come," Mirabelle said leading him to the couch. She looked up at Meiser to be sure that was an okay place to sit—she was so dang polite!

"Sure, great choice, Mirabelle—Stewart will be able to have room to sit next to you," Meiser praised her.

Another blush—I might have to keep this guy under lock and key.

I sat in the chair next to the couch and Meiser walked back to get Stewart. He came carrying him out, and I felt my shoulders tighten.

Mirabelle made the softest, sweetest, "Oooh—he is *so* cute!" She reached up to pet him. "What happened to his eye?" She sounded like she could cry.

Meiser had told Mirabelle about Stewart's eye, but she had probably forgotten and would remember now that she saw him.

Meiser told her he had been abused as a small kitten.

"No." Mirabelle inhaled and put her hands to her mouth.

"Mirabelle, it's okay, I promise. You just wait until he gets used to you and Spy—you will see that you don't have to be sad for him. He's very ornery," Meiser said.

Mirabelle hesitantly nodded.

Spy sat obediently. His jowls began to drool slightly, watching his Mirabelle with another animal.

Meiser walked around and sat down with Stewart, with Spy between him and Mirabelle. He let the two animals sniff each other—the universal animal approval system.

Stewart reached a small white paw out to tap Spy on his head playfully, and Spy made a small yelp while looking like he was smiling.

We all laughed, and Stewart wriggled out of Meiser's arms to move toward Mirabelle to her complete glee. Spy just sat happily.

"Well, I think I was worried for no reason," I said, standing to walk behind the couch with Meiser.

He grinned and turned on a Netflix kid's show that Mirabelle liked and went to get drinks and snacks for her. I stayed put, making sure no issues arose with the animals, and when Meiser got back, I went to get Spy's food and got some food for Stewart too. Meiser brought some iced tea out for the two of us at the dining room table so we could keep our eyes on the three of them.

"Thanks for bringing them over. Stewart gets lonely, I think," Meiser said.

"You need to adopt another cat," I said.

"Should I get three more like someone I know?"

I laughed. "You don't need to be the crazy cat guy or anything."

"How'd your big-time meeting go with the mayor of Tri-City, madame?" He switched gears when he saw the look on my face.

"Not good at all. He wants me to help him get

Delilah and her parents to sell the art district to him or some guy named Nestle—I have no idea exactly what is going on. Bradley said earlier that Nestle was involved with Lou. You don't think he could be involved in Lou's murder, do you?"

"We're looking at many angles of what could have happened," Meiser said, putting on his detective straight face.

"It just seems that the mayor and this Nestle guy are the ones behind the urban sprawl rumors and now Nestle is tied to Lou—maybe it's all connected," I said. "Do you think there could be anything illegal going on?"

Meiser jumped up from his seat. He lost his balance and fell into the counter that led to his kitchen. I lunged forward to reach for him, but he pushed me away. "I'm fine—I'm going to go get a snack, and if you don't mind, I don't want to talk work anymore tonight." He took a moment to get his balance and headed for the kitchen.

I sat silently, feeling like I had just been dismissed. When he came back, I excused myself and went to the restroom to get my bearings.

I splashed some water on my face to collect myself and noticed a prescription on his counter called Gilenya. I couldn't help but pick it up and wondered if this had to do with his stumbling. I had no clue what this was for. I had felt bad because when I first met him last year, I thought he was stumbling because he drank a lot. As I got to know him better, that thought left my head, and I guess I chose to ignore the stumbling until now. I needed to make a mental note to look this up.

I was getting ready to type it in my phone when I heard something at the window. His bathroom window had film over it so I couldn't immediately look out. I cracked the window but couldn't see anything.

I went back out. Meiser had made us a snack of cheese and crackers. "I know I don't make as elaborate snacks as you do, but this is the best I have."

"This is great," I said. "I'm sorry if I upset you."

"No, I'm sorry. I was rude. This case is getting to me. Every time we have a lead, it goes nowhere," he said.

I looked at the time. "Well, let's do what you said and change the topic—I thought we could order pizza for dinner before I have to take Mirabelle home."

"Pizza?" Mirabelle turned around with Stewart in her arms and Spy's head on her leg.

It looked like we had a satisfied customer.

Meiser went to pickup the pizza and I took the plates the cheese and crackers were on in the kitchen to clean them.

I was looking for baggies to put the crackers and cheese in when I heard Spy growling in the other room.

"Mirabelle, is everything alright in there?" I had been bent down head inside a cabinet. She didn't answer me.

"Mirabelle!" I yelled louder, getting up.

I walked to the front room and saw Stewart sitting on the couch alone.

"Mirabelle?" I ran back to the bathroom, then the bedroom. She wasn't in either place. I ran back to the front door and swung it open.

She wasn't out front.

"Mirabelle!" I yelled, jerking my head each way. My nerves were shot but I didn't have time to break down. I had to find that kid and her dog!

Meiser pulled into the drive and opened the garage door. When he saw me, he stopped the car and jumped out.

"What's going on?"

"I can't"—I inhaled and exhaled—"I can't."

He stared at me.

"Is the pizza here?" Mirabelle asked, walking out of the garage with Spy like nothing was up.

"Where on earth were you?" I yelled. I saw the expression change on her face, and I regrouped. "I'm sorry, Mirabelle. I didn't mean to yell. You really scared me. I couldn't find you."

"I'm sorry, Miss Jolie. Spy was growling at the door. I thought he wanted out. We went outside and were walking around, and Mr. Mick's door was open, so we went in for an adventure!"

"What door was open?" Meiser asked. "I just opened my garage door."

"Not the big door, the small one on the side," Mirabelle said. "Spy kept growling."

"Jolie, you take them inside. I'm going to look around, then I'll bring the pizza in."

"Pizza!" Mirabelle squeaked.

I took them in and set them back up at the TV and had my phone ready to dial. Then I realized Meiser was police.

He came back in and shrugged his shoulders. "Nothing missing and no one out there. I didn't think I'd left that door open, but I was outside working in the yard today. Grab some plates and let's eat!"

Chapter Thirteen

The next morning, I called Star and we scheduled to meet that afternoon to discuss cross-selling. I had a busy morning of prepping for the dinner special that night—chicken marsala done in the Dutch cast iron pot.

"Hey, I'm going to go over to M&M's Italian restaurant in a bit to meet with Star and maybe Olive about cross-selling," I told Ava.

"Do you really want to waste your time on those two? They weren't very welcoming before," she said.

"I don't know—they are a newer business and trying to get everything up and running. You remember what we were like when we started. We should give them a break. Plus, it sounds like we will need all the friends we can get with this whole urban sprawl thing looming over the village," I said.

"Delilah said that Nestle guy had approached her parents too," Ava huffed.

"I want to do something about it. I don't know what, though—should we talk to Mayor Nalini?" I asked.

"Maybe, something definitely needs to be done, though," Ava said.

Star was waiting for me at the bar when I arrived. She smiled warmly at me as I walked up to take the stool.

"Thanks for coming to me today. We are short on staff at the moment, and I didn't want to leave," she said.

"No problem, I appreciate you taking the opportunity to hear me out."

"Now, about this cross-selling—what did you have in mind?"

We were interrupted by Olive raising her voice up front. Star moved quickly to her sister's side and I followed. The Zimmerman brothers were towering over poor Olive and Zander was pointing a meaty finger in her face.

"I'm giving you one last chance to tell us what is going on here," Zander yelled.

"Sir, like I said before, I do not know what you are referring to. I am asking you politely to leave," Olive said not backing down and walking toward the brothers ushering them to the door.

"What is going on here?" Star's tone was heated.

"We want to know who this Milano character is and how he ties into Tri-City wanting to buy out land in Leavensport," Zander halted in place.

"Star, I'm handling this," Olive pleaded.

Star looked ready for war, "It's none of your business who owns this place. The only thing you brutes need to know is that my sister and I manage it. The land's for sale—anyone can buy it. Get over yourselves!"

Zed grabbed his brother's arm and pulled him out the door, but not before Zander spit an ugly glop of brownish-green spit all over their nice carpet.

"You'll pay for that, you Neanderthal!" Star screamed at them.

Olive shook her sister and shushed her.

"I'm so sorry you had to witness that unpleasantness," Olive said to me. "You two head back to the bar to finish your meeting. I'll work on getting this cleaned up."

"Make sure you get a picture and document the date and time. Jolie, you're a witness to what they did!" Star said hands shaking from rage.

"I've never seen the Zimmerman brothers show signs of rage before—but between the town meeting and today, it's a bit concerning," I said.

"A bit?" Star stood wide-eyed staring at me like I was nuts.

"Star, she's known them longer than we have. They could be having a bad time of it right now. Just take a breath and finish your meeting," Olive said.

"Sorry about that," Star said motioning for us to go back to our stools. "What were we talking about?"

"The cross-selling, I don't have to dictate it—you can decide if you have anything on your menu that could work in any of the shops in the village and if anything at the shops work in here to sell. It's just a way to help each other sell products while remaining a tight-knit community," I said happy to change the subject.

"No wonder Mick is infatuated with you," she

said.

I felt the dynamic change back a bit with that comment. "I don't know that I'd say he's infatuated," I said.

"I would say that. Mick is a good guy, but you don't know everything about him yet. I just hope you are in the relationship for the right reasons," she said, looking me dead in the eye.

"We've only started to date recently, Star—what are the right reasons in your opinion?" I asked, nervous from the confrontation.

"Well, there is a bit of an age difference there and you have to know that he may be looking for something more permanent, while you may just be looking to have some fun," she said, as my mouth opened in protest. She held up her hands. "Listen, I'm not saying there is anything wrong with a girl your age wanting nothing but fun—it's just that Mick may not see it that way, and I'm looking out for him as a friend."

I wanted to give her my two cents about her comments, but I remembered that she had been upset recently with the first anniversary of her mom's death and bit my tongue. Also, she just had that crazy scene with the Zimmermans, "Listen, I have no intentions of hurting Meiser."

"You can't even call him by his first name!" Star exclaimed.

"I'm sorry, Star, I don't want to talk about this anymore. I feel like you are purposely picking a fight with me and I've heard about what your mom went through last year, and I can't imagine what you are feeling. I don't want to argue with you," I said, hoping that would defuse the situation.

WRONG! At first, Star looked melancholy, but

then her face altered a bit and she turned on me. "Who told you what happened? I don't even know that anyone knows the entire story but me and Olive, and I *know* she wouldn't tell you!" she exclaimed defensively.

"No, I don't think I know the whole story. Gaze told Delilah you were sad, and she shared with me that your mom had a stroke and passed away. I'm so sorry. She had to be so young," I said.

At the mention of Gaze, Star calmed down. "Thanks, I'm sorry I flew off the handle there," she said in a softer voice. "It was all unexpected and seemed to happen in a blur. It was all bad enough, but she had to be in this horrible nursing home. The staff was completely incompetent—there was no reason she had to die." She stared off at the wall like she had forgotten I was there.

"What do you mean?" I asked, reaching for her hand in comfort, but she jerked it away and changed the subject.

"Gaze is such a great kid—I want the best for her in life," she said.

"That she is—very creative too," I said.

"Yep, well, I'll take what you said to Olive, and we'll look around the village and make some decisions on what to cross-sell and get back to you soon," she said, ending the meeting.

When I got back to the restaurant, Ava said to me, "Well, you were gone long enough to miss the lunch rush *again*."

Okay, so maybe she was right, and I needed to get my priorities straight, but I couldn't resist saying, "Hey, I was at a business meeting, you know?"

"Mmm hmmm, and how did that meeting go, your highness?" Ava asked, looking at Delilah, who was sitting at the counter. Ava walked around the counter and put a finger up pointing to customers while she held the coffeepot.

I took it from her getting her drift. "Here, let me, since I haven't been working my share amount lately." Ava rolled her eyes at Delilah, who just giggled under her breath. I was filling up Dr. Libby's cup and chatting with her about how my cats were doing and telling her I'd be bringing Lenny in soon for his annual check-up when Meiser walked in and smiled at me. Unfortunately, he walked in while I was filling her cup and I looked up and got caught up in his hotness and coffee overflowed.

"Whoa, I do need caffeine but not a vat of it, Jolie," Dr. Libby said with her hearty laugh.

"Sorry," I mumbled as Ava rushed over with a wet towel to wipe it up. Mirabelle smiled at Meiser from the front of the restaurant.

"Looks like someone's got a crush," Dr. Libby said.

"Oh, I think she's got way more than a crush," Ava said, giving me a knowing look.

"No, I meant Mirabelle," Dr. Libby said, pointing.

"Not her too? What is it with this man?" Ava asked.

"I can't say I blame them," Dr. Libby said, smiling at me and winking.

We got everything cleaned up and moved to the counter with Delilah and Meiser. Delilah ordered some coconut chai hot tea with two sweeteners and a few drops of milk. Meiser loved my mocha cold drinks, which I kept in the back fridge just for me and asked for one.

"So, Mr. Detective, I went over to your girlfriend's this morning, and she had her door unlocked again," Ava told Meiser.

I shook my head—she was always giving me a hard time about having my doors unlocked. "I forgot my garage door was up!"

"What does that have to do with anything?" Meiser asked.

"First off, I only leave my doors unlocked when I'm home. And, when my garage door is down, it's no biggie to leave the door unlocked, but I forgot I had to go out through the garage this morning to grab the weekly advertiser before it rained. I forgot to close the garage door and left the door unlocked," I said.

"Still makes no sense to me," Meiser said.

"Now I am starting to get why people like you," Ava said.

Meiser smiled at her and said, "You live alone— you need to keep your doors locked."

"They are locked when I leave the house and when it's dark. I really don't think this is anyone's business," I said, sticking my head out toward Ava.

"Please don't say because we live in a safe village with everything going on lately," Delilah chimed in.

"Okay, point taken," I said.

"Gotta get to work," Meiser said and leaned across the counter to kiss me.

"YOWZA," Ava said, fanning her face with her hand. "You two are getting hot and heavy."

I wish she would have waited to yell that after Meiser left. His body jerked, but he was kind enough to not turn around in acknowledgment and kept moving out of the restaurant.

"You know, it looks like Star and Olive will participate in the village's cross-selling after all," I said. "She shared a little with me about her mom's death, but I don't understand it all—she was all over the place with being angry, sad, and then she calmed down once I brought up Gaze. She loves her niece a lot."

"I love getting to work with Gaze. She's a super-sweet kid," Delilah said. "Ava told me you were asking about some of the projects on display with the cut-out letters."

"Oh yeah, it just stood out to me because I got a letter that looked like that," I said nervously, hoping Delilah wouldn't think I blamed her, as Ava had.

"Some of my students struggle with spelling, reading, or writing, so I find that cutting out letters and helping them sound out each letter helps. Gaze struggles with dyslexia, so she is one I have helped," Delilah said.

"Wow, that's a great idea," I said.

"I'd love to take credit for it, but I talked to some of the teachers at our school district, and they gave me lots of great ideas to help that directly involve texture."

"My girl is wicked smart—and brave," Ava said.

"Brave?" I questioned.

"Yeah, I decided I'm not selling no matter what. My parents are going with whatever I decide, since they already have me managing all the shops and the two I don't own will go to me through inheritance. So, come what may, even if they do drive me out of business," Delilah said, sitting up straighter.

Mirabelle walked up and said, "Miss Jolie, can I get some water for Spy, please?"

"Of course, girl—let's go back to the kitchen and get you something too," Ava said. Mirabelle knew we couldn't let Spy back in the kitchen or behind the counter, so she handed Spy off to me and took Ava's arm so she could lead her back.

"I wanted to tell you again how sorry I am for ruining your first date with Detective Meiser." Delilah reached across the counter and grabbed my hand.

"No apologies necessary, truly—I felt like I was a bad friend to Ava because I didn't go to check on her," I said.

"You know her better than anyone—she needed space. I hurt her, and I feel horrible about that," she said, looking down at her lap.

"Couples argue. You know Ava loves you. She was thrilled when Bradley asked to walk over to check on you yesterday," I said.

"He's the one who asked to come and check on me?" Delilah's eyes brimmed with tears.

"Yeah, she wanted to call you to let you know she knew what was wrong and he asked her to go over with him to check on you." I smiled.

Ava led Mirabelle out of the kitchen with one arm, holding a huge bowl of ice cream with all kinds of yummy toppings for Mirabelle—she was carefully carrying Spy's bowl of water.

"Where do you two want to eat?" I asked.

"Can we sit outside at one of the tables?" Mirabelle asked.

"I heard you got to meet a new kitty the other

night," Delilah told Mirabelle.

She turned around quickly. Her round face lit up with excitement and her cheeks were rosier than usual. "He was so cute and sweet. He and Spy got along great. Spy is the best doggie ever," she said, bending down to hug Spy. "Okay, I need to go outside and eat my ice cream now before it melts," she said, and with that, the two took off. Magda walked over to carry the ice cream and water for them.

"Hey, I need to head out too, but are the two of you coming to the Dotting the Eyes art event for the kids to showcase their work so far this summer?" Delilah asked.

"Wouldn't miss it. We have your order and will have it all ready and bring it," Ava said.

I pulled into my garage after a long day. I couldn't wait to get inside my air-conditioned house, change clothes, do my normal kitty chores, and sit down to relax. I closed the garage door and thought to lock my door after being reamed by Meiser and Ava.

I bent down to say hello to my greeters, filled their food bowls and gave them fresh water, cleaned out the litter boxes, and ran upstairs to change into cutoff sweats and a tank top.

I sat down at the kitchen table to look through my latest cast iron magazine issue in peace with my sweetened iced tea. I heard something strange and thought it must be one of the cats scratching on something, but when I looked around, I didn't see them. I did see the doorknob of the door from the garage moving as though someone were twisting it. I moved quietly to the counter and grabbed my phone. I called Meiser to whisper what was happening.

"Hey, good looking," he said into the phone.

"Someone is trying to break into my house right now," I whispered. I felt like the intruder could hear my heart pounding. I looked around, contemplating what to do. I could run out the front door, but I didn't know if there was more than one intruder and I didn't want to leave my cats here alone.

"Stay on the phone with me. I was at Kwani's gas station, so I'm only a minute or two out. Go find someplace to hide until I get there," Meiser said evenly.

"It sounds like they are trying to jimmy the lock," I said.

"I told you to go hide," he said again, but I had another idea.

"I'm on the phone with Detective Meiser, and he is on my street right now coming here!" I yelled through the door.

"Jolie," Meiser said sternly.

"They stopped," I said. He started to say something else, and I shushed him. "I don't hear anything," I said worriedly.

"I'm here; stay in there," he said.

A few minutes later, there was a knock on my door from the garage.

"It's me, Jolie," Meiser yelled.

I opened the door slowly.

"They ran out your side door to the garage. It was open when I got here. I didn't find anyone but don't come out here or touch anything. I've called it in," he said.

"Do you think someone was at your house last

night?"

"If I wasn't thinking that before, I am now," he said.

Chapter Fourteen

"What's going on? Why was the chief telling me I couldn't come into your house?" Ava harrumphed, hands on hips. She looked out of breath.

"Someone tried to break in—I called Meiser, but they got away," I said, still pacing from adrenaline.

"Teddy is just doing his job, Ava—they need to dust for prints and look to see if they can find anything the intruder may have left behind," Meiser said. "I see you pushed *your* way through," he said as an afterthought.

"I have my ways," she said mysteriously. "So they don't know who it was?"

"No, did you see anything? They ran out the side door of the garage that is by your house," I said.

"I was watching *Housewives of New Jersey*," Ava said.

"So she heard and saw nothing," I said to Meiser.

All of a sudden, my entire family rushed in the door with the chief following.

"Meiser, do you think you can keep them all in here, since I can't seem to keep them from coming in?" Teddy asked.

"No one is leaving here anytime soon. You just go do your job," Grandma Opal said. Only she could get away with scolding the chief of police.

"That's what I thought I was trying to do," Chief Tobias said.

"Don't sass me, young man, I knew you when you were in diapers—that badge may impress some people, but not me," Grandma Opal spit out, galloping over to me.

"Is my girl okay?" Grandma asked as my mother stood there looking devastated.

"I'm fine, Mom," I said, looking past Grandma to Mom. My grandma and mom loved each other, but they didn't always like each other. Mother/daughter things from way back. I knew my mom was worried about my safety—so was my grandma, but my grandma and Aunt Fern both had a taste for overdramatizing everything.

My mom shook her head and turned around. A tear fell from her face as she reached to wipe it. Meiser walked over to her with a tissue.

"Grandma, I said I'm fine." I swatted her hand away. She was checking me over as if someone had attacked me. "No one got in—everyone relax. I'm starved," I said. I wasn't really hungry, but I knew that would make my grandma and Aunt Fern switch gears to cook so I could breathe. I didn't like people hovering over me.

"Fernie, look in the fridge, and I'll check the cabinets to see what she has. What about everyone else? Should we fix dinner for everyone?" Grandma looked to Uncle Wylie, Mom, Meiser, and Ava, who all nodded in agreement.

"Just make sure you have all the ingredients

here," Meiser said. "You can't leave while they are outside working."

Aunt Fern sashayed up to Meiser and rubbed her hand up and down his bicep. "We understand, Detective." Aunt Fern loved the men.

"Fernie, leave him alone," my mom barked.

Meiser's eyes widened and he grinned at me.

"You are a handsome fella," Grandma Opal said. "I don't mind listening to you, but that Teddy—I'm not too happy with him right now," she said, grabbing two boxes of macaroni and telling Aunt Fern to take some ground chuck from the freezer and to thaw it while she grabbed some tomato sauce, basil, garlic, oil, and other goodies to make what looked like Marzetti.

"What did Teddy do to you now?" I asked, referring to last fall when she was upset with him over the murder.

"Well, first off, I have a bunch of grocery bags out in the car for you, but I can't bring them in now," she said, referring to the bags I used to line the trash cans by each litter box.

"What did you do, Grandma?" I asked, feeling like I could only take so much more today.

"Nothing, I was at Costello's and went through the self-checkout. I triple bagged everything to give you some bags for the kitty boxes. When I went to take a bag of groceries, the whole stack of bags pulled off the rack," she said, turning away to stir the pasta in the salted, oiled water.

"She stole a bunch of bags for you," Uncle Wylie said, laughing. Uncle Wylie was the opposite of the women in our family. We were all uptight and let things fester inside. He let everything roll off his back, and he thought we were all hilarious. He had the best laugh too. His eyes always filled with tears and lit up when he did his throaty laugh and slapped his hand on his knee.

"Grandma, I don't need you to steal bags for me!" I said in a whisper-yell.

Ava had chipmunk cheeks trying not to laugh, and Meiser looked like he was enjoying the local circus performances right in my very own kitchen!

"I didn't steal them. It's not my fault if the entire stack came out—and you know that Mr. Costello has always had it out for me since I turned him down for a date in high school," she said, still not facing me.

"I think he is over what happened in high school, Mom, especially since he's been married twice now with kids and grandkids," my mom said.

"Well, what do you call ratting me out to the chief?" she snapped.

"So, you were in jail again?" I asked.

"No, but the chief came and made me give the bags back." Grandma's face scrunched up in anger.

"Don't steal for me," I said.

Meiser touched my arm, knowing I was getting too worked up with the events of the evening.

"Food's ready," Uncle Wylie said, always being the mediator between the women in the family.

When we sat down, I pushed my curls behind my ears and rubbed my hands on my legs. I looked over and saw Meiser watching me.

My mom must have caught the entire scene and said, "She's always done that since she was a toddler."

Meiser looked over at her quizzically.

"Push the hair behind the ears and rub her legs—she gets nervous around a lot of people, especially when the topic of conversation is her," Patty said.

"This one's always been shy," Grandma Opal said, pointing her thumb at me. "The family always wanted to take her out on her birthday and have the staff sing happy birthday to her, and she would get so red in the face and angry. She'd throw a temper tantrum every time we got home, and we eventually stopped doing it."

We all stopped talking and finished eating, mainly because I didn't have a table large enough for all of us and some had to sit in the living room, the island, and the table.

After cleanup, I moved chairs into the living room so we all could fit.

"So, who is Jolie staying with tonight?" my mom asked.

"I don't need to stay with anyone," I said. "Plus, I'm not leaving the cats here alone."

"Okay, fair enough, then who is staying with you?" Meiser said.

"Are you offering?" Aunt Fern elbow-nudged him.

"I don't mind sleeping on the couch," Meiser said.

"What about Stewart?" I said.

"I can bring him over," he said.

"I can stay over tonight," Uncle Wylie said. Since my biological father was mostly MIA and my stepdad had passed away, he had taken over the role of father figure, and I could tell he wasn't comfortable with Meiser staying over. "I'll stay in your guest room."

"Sounds good," I said. I really didn't want to be alone tonight—the truth was, I had no idea who was doing this or why. Also, I didn't know if it was connected to Lou's murder or not.

"Ava told us about your meeting with Delilah," Aunt Fern said. "So, is Lou's murder messed up in all this?" she asked, looking at Meiser.

Uh-oh, I hoped he didn't treat her the way he treated me.

"Possibly," he said.

"I know the Seevers and the Zimmermans were suspects for a time," Uncle Wylie said.

"I can't see any of them doing anything like that. I don't care if Lou swindled them out of money—they've lived in the village forever and have been friends with Lou for so long. I can't imagine any of them beating him, let alone killing him," Ava said.

"Me neither," I said.

"I heard that Lou was poisoned—he took a regular prescription, and someone swapped out the pills and that the beating happened after he was dead," Ava said.

"Who told you all that?" Meiser demanded angrily.

Ava took a moment to think before she spoke—which was unusual. "I heard it in the restaurant—you know—village gossip."

Meiser didn't look convinced.

"If that's true, then someone had to really hate him," my mom said.

"Yeah, but it could have been someone who didn't want to chance getting hurt by him and did it to get satisfaction after the fact," I said. "Or someone not strong enough to beat him to death but that's what they wanted to do."

Meiser looked at me appreciatively.

"I Spy—" Ava started as everyone stared.

I quickly interrupted, "Wasn't there a story on the news recently about someone being poisoned in assisted living or something?"

"I don't remember hearing anything like that," Grandma Opal said.

There was a knock on my front door. "Hey, Teddy," I said, opening the door for him to come in. "Want some Johnny Marzetti? We have plenty left over."

Teddy never turned down food. "Of course," he said, walking to my kitchen and grabbing a bowl and filling it up. I grew up with him, Ava, Keith, Lydia, Betsy, and Bradley, so we were all pretty comfortable around each other, even though we didn't always get along at times.

"So, we found no fingerprints, meaning they had gloves on," he said, then took a bite of food, saw Uncle Wylie, smiled, and walked over to shake his hand. Teddy's dad had been the chief, and his dad was my uncle's best friend until he was shot and killed on duty. Uncle Wylie fathered many of us.

"How's it going, Teddy?" Uncle Wylie asked.

"Real good, Wylie." He took another bite, then looked at Meiser. "We did find a cut-out letter in the grass out back, though."

"Do you think this is tied into Lou or the urban sprawl?" Meiser asked.

"Hard to tell," Teddy said.

Meiser rushed outside and I moved to the window to see what he was doing. He looked in my mailbox but came back empty-handed.

"I wonder if whoever was trying to break in knew you were here, Jolie?" Ava asked.

"I don't know—I was sitting quietly at the table when I saw the doorknob moving and then I tried to be quiet when I called Meiser, but when I yelled, they stopped and ran," I said.

"I'd feel better if I knew whether they knew you were here or not," Ava said.

"Me too," Meiser said.

Me too, I thought.

Chapter Fifteen

The next day we were at the restaurant prepping food for Delilah's Dotting the Eyes art event that evening. I was mixing the cornbread batter when I heard Ava's voice rise out front.

Nestle, the man who had been at Delilah's shop, was out front. Ava was right up in his face. She pushed him on his chest, yelling, "Uh-uh—no way—GET OUT!" Other patrons stopped eating, their forks midway in the air.

Nestle grinned at her. "I'm not threatening you or anything. I'm only asking if you'd help me talk to your girlfriend into doing the right thing for your village. Plus, I'm thinking about sitting down and trying some of this delicious food I've heard about. I mean, if I'm going to own the shops next to you, I'm sure I'll be over here regularly to eat—unless some better restaurants are built at the other side of town."

The Zimmerman brothers happened to be eating at our restaurant, and both got up with their dirty bib overalls. They towered over Nestle in his suit and tie. Zed rubbed at his long straggly beard with calloused hands and looked eagerly at Nestle. "All of us that live here have known each other pretty near our entire lives—small community and all. We don't take too kindly to outsiders coming in and threatening us," he said, taking two steps forward while Zander moved to the other side of Nestle. This was one time I was happy to have the men be intimidating.

I walked over to Mirabelle, whose eyes were bulging, and breaths were raspy due to the confrontation. "You get out and leave us alone!" Mirabelle yelled. Spy lunged forward, growling at Nestle.

"Mirabelle, thank you, but you don't need to be involved in this sweetie, okay? Here, I see you are doing some coloring—why don't you color this part green?" I said, looking to Ava to get her to take care of this.

Zed saw my look and grabbed Nestle by the arm to remove him from the restaurant. "Hands off me. I get it. I'm not wanted here—for now. I'll leave," Nestle said, stomping out.

Mirabelle stuck her tongue out at him as he left.

Nestle stopped with the door partially open and turned around. "You know, maybe we will leave your girlfriend alone. Come to think of it; we could just buy up a bunch of acres and put our own art district and restaurants and one of everything this village has and run you all out of business." He strutted back in and up to the counter and grabbed one of our to-go menus. "This will be great research for a cast iron restaurant," he said as he walked out.

Ava and I gave each other a leery look.

Nestle had unhinged everyone with his threats

earlier. Now, at home getting ready for the art event that evening, I hated that I didn't feel safe or comfortable in my home. I was constantly on edge.

I changed into linen slacks and a short-sleeved blouse and sandals. Ava had all the food, and we were driving over together. Last fall, we'd invested in an alarm for our restaurant—now I was thinking of getting one for my little cottage. Worse than my own fear for myself, I was afraid to leave the cats alone. What if the intruder would have let them out or hurt them?

One thing I did do was change the code on my garage door. Uncle Wylie had also put deadbolts on every door and a chain on top of the regular lock the night before. It was something.

I was double-checking all the locks when the phone rang. I figured it was Ava, reminding me to bring something.

But it was the same voice from last week. "Best not to attend the event tonight or else you'll find out what could have happened to you last night at your house before the detective showed up."

Anger coursed through my body and I threw my phone across the room into the wall. Every part of my body trembled. I was furious that this person was hiding behind a distorted voice app and trying to dictate my life.

My poor cats ran upstairs. I took a few deep breaths and got myself together. I ran upstairs using my best kitty squeaky voice. "Hey, babies, want some 'momma is sorry for being nuts' extra treatsas for today?" At the word "treatsas," which is what I say for "treats," they all came to me and followed me downstairs. "Treatsas, Treatsas, Treatsas—what kitty cats are ready for treats, treat-

treat-treat, treat-treat-treat, treat-treat-treat—they eat their treats, eat their treats, eat their treats," I sang in a high-pitched voice like a kid's song. I loved turning every song into a cat song and made up songs for my cats all the time. I was a true cat lady.

I told Ava what had happened on the way to Crafty's Corner.

"Why are you going? Turn around and go home—I'll drive myself over. Delilah won't care," she said.

"No, I'm not letting this jerk ruin my life. I'm sick of living in fear. Also, the use of Meiser being my 'boyfriend' really bothers me," I said.

"You two are in a relationship," Ava said.

"No, I know—that's not what I mean. It's just—I don't know what it is—the voice was distorted—but it was the tone that makes me feel like I should know who it is," I said.

"Who is it?" Ava said.

"I don't know—I can't place it," I said. "Ava, it's everything—the threat of urban sprawl—the town reaction to it—threats to me—financial fraud—cut-out letters—distorted voices—poisoned pills—it all feels familiar, but I can't place it."

"None of it rings true for me," Ava said.

"That picture you took of the land with the vial of blue liquid. Do you think it was some sort of poison? I want it to be directly tied to Mayor Cardinal and Nestle—I feel like they have a hand in it—but I'm not sure if they do or not," I said.

"They definitely have a hand in the urban sprawl—we know that!" Ava exclaimed.

"True, but like Mayor Nalini said, it's not

illegal—unless there is corruption over buying the land."

Chapter Sixteen

The Leavensport art district was in the northwest part of the village—right across from Cast Iron Creations. The buildings were made of bricks and there was a raised marble-looking sidewalk. There were no roads for cars to travel down this little part of the village—it was open only to pedestrians and cyclists.

Crafty's Corner had the appearance of a barn, but it was done in stone and two stories tall. There was green grass all around it with red mulch and beautiful flowers and a vegetable garden the kids helped to grow. Trees and bushes surrounded the property.

Even though the outside was cheerful, I loved the inside more because it was entirely decorated by the kids and artists who inhabited the space. Cubbyholes were painted in bright colors with names and pictures drawn and hung on them. Tonight, Delilah had the entire place clean, which was opposite of the normal chaos of projects in process. When customers walked in, they would see a store selling all kinds of art and craft supplies, as well as kids' and artists' finished pieces for sale.

This room led back to the work area, where the magic took place. From that room, there was a hallway with some of the best work displayed leading to a showcase room—this room had its own entrance from the side of the building. The back part of the room had an extra wall for a showcase that didn't extend the full length of the room. Those of us who knew Delilah well knew we could walk around that wall and there was an employee section in the back with a door leading to the alley, where the dumpsters were. Ava parked back there so we could get the food in easily without disturbing the villagers entering from the side to see their kids' art pieces.

We walked in with no food at first and found that several people were already there, including Mayor Cardinal, Nestle, Star, Olive, Gaze, the Seevers, the Zimmermans, and the crew who I grew up with, as well as a few others. Delilah gave us directions on where to set up the food and then asked if Ava could go with her momentarily.

I headed out back to grab a warmer bag filled with cast iron made goodies, but Keith grabbed my arm and pulled me to the side.

"Hey, how are you? I heard about someone trying to break in," he said.

"A little shaken, but I'm okay," I said.

"Listen, I really need to talk to you about something important," he said.

"Okay, well, I need to get the food first. Can I find you in a little while? I didn't realize so many people would already be here," I said.

"That's fine, but don't wait too long—it's serious," he said. "Find me as soon as you get a chance."

I pulled two warmers of food out of the trunk of the car and headed to the back door, but it was locked. This was weird, seeing as we just walked in this way and it was unlocked. I took a breath and sucked it up. I was going to have to carry the food around to the side and make sure it was unlocked when we came back out.

I began walking down the alley and got to a point where there wasn't as much light, which really stunk as it was dark out now. At first, I thought I had tripped on something until my head smashed into the brick walk. Someone had shoved me hard, and the warmers with the food flew out of my hands. I wasn't able to think fast enough to use my hands to help block my fall and fell face first.

I felt scrapes on my hands but used them to try and push up a little. I shook my head back and forth, still trying to figure out what happened. Someone kicked me in my stomach and sent me back flat on the ground as all the breath left me and pain screamed out in my hip. I felt as if I were slithering like a snake on the ground—anything to move forward toward the light on the side of the building. I could see it in reach. I wanted to scream, but the impact of the fall and the kick was so intense that I wasn't able to at that moment.

I continued my serpentine method of movement, bumping my body off some rocks on the ground and the raised sidewalk to continue moving forward. Suddenly, I felt the thug grab a huge handful of my curls and lift my head back. I saw the curb of the sidewalk and imagined my face getting slammed into it. Then it came—that survivor's instinct that people in traumatic situations say will kick in. The noise bellowed from the depth of my soul—I screamed bloody murder in complete terror and heard the side door slam. The brute let go of me and took off in the dark.

I curled inside myself, shaking all over and sobbing, unable to catch my breath. I felt battered and bruised, but that was nothing compared to the vulnerability of my sanity.

"My God, Jolie, what happened?" Ava came running at me and grabbed me and wrapped me in her arms as she sat on the sidewalk that had almost rearranged my face. She rocked me back and forth, then reached for her phone and called Delilah. She told her to send Teddy or Meiser or guys out back now.

Keith and Bradley came flying around the corner. "What happened?" they yelled in unison.

Ava, normally the loudest in the room, shushed them and whispered, "You're okay now, sister—just breathe, sweetie—I've got you; I've got you."

I cried into her chest and let her mother me.

An ambulance showed up moments later, and before I knew it I was at the hospital, and my family, Meiser, and Ava were there. Lydia refused to allow any other nurses to look after me, even though she wasn't on duty. Our love/hate frenemy relationship had switched back to love for the moment.

"You really need to learn to mind your own business," she said testily to me when it was only the two of us and she was checking me over.

"All I did was go to get the food for the Dotting the Eyes art event," I said.

"Somehow I don't think that's all you've done. You've angered someone trying to figure out who the murderer is or who's behind the urban sprawl—right?" she asked, hands on hips.

"Lydia, I don't have the energy right now," I said. I felt like I hadn't slept in years. I was so tired.

"Okay, you will need to take it easy."

"Hey, can I ask you a question? Have you heard of the medication Gilenya? Do you know what it's used for?"

"It's a drug for MS. Can I come in?" Meiser peeked in the room.

Lydia looked at me for an answer.

"Sure," I said lowering my brows.

"They ran some tests on her, and I double-checked everything," Lydia said. "Nothing is broken, but she does have bruised ribs. She's going to need to rest. Also, as her friend, I don't think she should be left alone until they figure out who is doing this."

"I agree. That's why I talked your family—even your Uncle Wylie—into allowing me to stay with you," Meiser told me.

"But what about—"

He interrupted me. "Stewart is currently on his way to your house now—I'll take care of integrating them or separate him if I need to. You don't need to worry about anything but rest."

"I'm sorry I snooped in your bathroom."

"I was going to tell you. We'll need to talk more about it, but right now, let's get you home."

Meiser helped me escape my family in the waiting room and got me to his truck.

"So, how did you talk my Uncle Wylie into letting you stay with me?" I asked.

"I told him I had a gun," he said, glancing at me

as he helped me into the car.

"That'll do it," I said, wincing as he put the seat belt around me. I felt his body flinch when he heard me grunt in pain.

He got in the truck, and we headed home.

"I wish I had been there with you when it happened. Or *if* I had been there, maybe—"

"Don't play what-if. Trust me—I'm the queen of what-iffing. It does no one any good," I said, looking out the window with tears in my eyes.

"Are you able to tell me what happened?" he asked carefully.

"Always the detective," I said. "You can't help yourself, can you?"

"Sorry," he said.

"It's okay. I don't want to go into all the details. But I will say that Ava and I went in the back and Delilah had the door unlocked so we could bring the food in that way. When I went out, the door was locked, which made me walk down the alley to the side entrance. I'm assuming someone in there walked back and locked the door, then came out the front and around the back to attack me."

"Okay, well, I'll be staying with you until we figure this out," he said.

"You can't stay with me twenty-four/seven," I said.

"I think between me, Ava, and your family that we have you covered," he said.

Grandma Opal's car was sitting in my drive when we got there.

"Oh, Lord," I said.

Meiser helped me out and into the house. He

asked what I'd normally do with the cats, and I told him. He went to do some house chores while my grandma made me some tea and sat in the chair next to the couch where I lay.

I felt bad because she looked so concerned, but I said, "Grandma, I hope you aren't going to ask me about the attack. I can't talk about it. I'm exhausted, and my mind has been on a constant loop of what happened." I was trying not to cry.

Bless my grandma's heart; she said, "I wasn't going to say anything, honey. I wanted to tell you about some of the art the kids made."

I smiled up at her and tried to pull the cover up. But she grabbed it from me and put it around me. She sat my head on her lap, rubbing her hand through my hair soothingly.

"The Zimmerman boy made puppets that look exactly like Zed and Zander. The long beards and hair with bib overalls and he added little legs with work boots and wait for it—" she said, laughing out loud. "He put cow dung on the bottom of the boots."

"No." I pushed up a little too fast and winced but couldn't help laughing while tears spilled out from pain. "Oh man, I would pay to see that!"

"Zed and Zander thought it was great," she said.

"I'll bet!" I exclaimed.

"Oh, and that Gaze, she is so cute, but that child must be a bit demented. She made this picture of unicorns with rainbows over them and added this eerie fire and brimstone around the unicorn. Kind of strange for a child, but maybe she is a child prodigy and will be an amazing artist later in life."

This time I jerked my body up and yelled in pain.

"Child, what is wrong with you! Be careful," Grandma yelled.

Meiser was walking back in when I yelled and walked over to me. "Do you need to get up? Here, let me help you."

"No, I need to adjust. I'm really tired," I said, hoping Grandma would take the hint.

"My cue to leave. You get some rest, honey. I'll take care of getting food to you tomorrow." She reached down and kissed me on the head and headed out.

"Walk her out, please," I looked up at Meiser.

I couldn't believe what my grandma had just said. Unicorns, rainbows, fire, and brimstone. Did Gaze make the picture?

As soon as Meiser walked back in, I said, "Listen to this—"

"I heard what she saw," he said.

"Do you know the entire story of Star and Olive's mom?" I asked.

"Their mom had a stroke, and at the time, she had a financial advisor. When she had the stroke, the guy took her money and ran. The girls couldn't afford proper care for her, and she was put in a not-so-great nursing home. She had to take a lot of pills, and she couldn't speak. One of the nurses gave her the wrong meds, and it killed her," Meiser said.

My mind was foggy from everything that had happened to me the last few days, but it was spinning. I felt my eyes go back and forth in thought and then noticed that Meiser's body had gone stiff.

We both realized at the same time—it was a similar story with Lou.

"What are you going to do?" I asked.

"Right now, I'm going to sleep. We don't know anything for certain. Tomorrow, I will look into it more when someone takes a shift with you," he said, helping me up.

"I'm sorry, I know they are your friends," I said.

He gently lifted me in his arms, and I put my arms around his neck.

"What are you doing?" I asked.

"Carrying you up to your room. You don't need to worry about the steps for now."

After Meiser carried me up and helped get my nightclothes placed where I could easily get into them, he stepped into the hall and shut the door. When I was done, he came back in and tucked me in bed.

"Do you think you'll be able to get to the bathroom okay?" he asked.

"Of course. I can call you if I need anything." I held my phone up.

"Yep, I'll be on the couch, and you can call my cell," he said.

"You can stay in the guest bedroom next door," I said.

"No, I'd rather stay on the first floor so I can hear if anyone attempts anything."

When he went downstairs, I thought I'd fall straight asleep. I didn't. My mind wandered all over the place, replaying the last two weeks. My gut told me it was Star. It's how her mood changed at our meeting and how defensive she got so quickly. Her emotions were all over the place.

I grabbed my phone and opened the credit card case where I stuffed business cards, finding the one

Star gave me.

I dialed her number and took a breath, waiting for her to answer. I got her voicemail.

Another breath and with a lighthearted voice, I said, "Hi Star, this is Jolie Tucker of Cast Iron Creations. I wanted to get back to you about the cross-selling. You will probably have heard about what happened to me by the time you get this message. I'll be at my house for a while, but I need to continue to work to keep my sanity. Would you be able to come over late tomorrow afternoon to meet with me so we can further discuss cross-selling? My address is 2201 Cherry Street. If you can make it between three and four that would be great. Thanks, bye."

Okay, tomorrow morning, I would let Meiser know that I thought it was Star and why, and that I had called her here. He could be in another room. I was pretty sure I could get her to confess.

I turned over and fell fast asleep.

Chapter Seventeen

I had taken some pain pills before I went to bed the night before. I normally dream and remember my dreams—but this time there were no dreams or none that I remembered. Meiser was lightly shaking me, trying to get me to wake up. I was groggy and trying to come to. My entire body felt like a Mack truck had run over me. Truthfully, I wasn't even sure it was the beating as much as the mental abuse I had gone through—all the TV shows, movies, and books always focus so much on the feel of the body when attacked. I knew firsthand that the physical pain was *much* less than the mental pain, which would never heal completely.

"Hey, Jolie, how are you this morning?" Meiser was smiling down at me—he had sat on the edge of the bed.

"I hurt," I said, incoherently using that word to describe body, soul, and spirit.

"Hey, you slept a long time, though. It's eleven thirty," he said.

I normally get up very early and, hearing the time, I tried to jerk my body up, but it wouldn't listen to me.

"Hey, no worries. Just rest. I came up here because I have to leave for just a couple of hours. Keith is downstairs—he needs to talk to you. I asked if he would stay with you until I got back. Do you want me to tell him you are going back to sleep?"

"No, will you help me put a robe on and help me down the steps?"

"Sure," he said gently reaching around my back and putting his arms under my armpits to carefully move me into an upright position. This is something I could have done on my own if I could have taken a bit of time to wake up, but I knew he needed to leave.

Meiser got my robe and helped to stand me up and get it on me. He went to pick me up again, and I said, "No, please help me walk to the steps, then I'll see if I can make it down—my body is all stoved up, and I need to move a little to help loosen it up," I said.

"Whatever you need," he said, letting me lean on him.

"Hey," I said, stopping for a moment and looking up at him. He looked down at me. "You have been so wonderful to me the last couple of weeks—no— the last several months. You've been patient, kind, funny, and caring. Whether you know it or not, you are treating me like a queen, and I wanted you to know I really appreciate it. I know I'm a handful and not an easy person to be around," I said with tears in my eyes.

He took what felt like an eternity and stared right into my eyes—into my soul—then said, "I've never had any luck with relationships. I know it has a lot to do with who I am as a person and my past.

There's so much you don't know about me, so maybe don't put me on a pedestal—but there is something different about you, Jolie. I can feel it in my bones. We share something—I don't even know if I know what it is yet. But I can tell you that I'm damn excited to find out."

He bent down to kiss me. I tried to raise my arms to his face but winced in pain and settled for putting my hands on his biceps.

We got to the steps and went a few steps down, and I didn't think I could make it. "Do you need me to carry you?" Meiser asked.

Keith came to the bottom of the steps and began moving up toward us. "Here, let me help."

Keith came to my other side, and the three of us were scrunched between the railings. I realized this would not work and we all laughed at once. What an awkward situation to literally be in between these two, but how refreshing that we could all laugh together.

Keith moved one step in front of me and told me to put my free hand on him and use him as a crutch to help my weight as I went down a step. That seemed to work well.

We got down the steps and Meiser reached down to kiss me. Out of the corner of my eye, I saw Keith turn his head.

"Do you need anything done—can I get you something to drink or eat or do you need to take pills? Meiser said something about pain pills," Keith said nervously after Meiser had left.

"Um," I said, rubbing my head. "Sorry, I'm groggy—I need pain pills and caffeine, but I'm supposed to eat something with the pills—also— Mick probably already did this, but can you check the litter boxes and make sure the cats have food?" Then I realized how much I was asking. "I'm sorry for asking you to do so much when you came to talk to me." I slumped my shoulders—I felt so helpless right now.

"No problem at all, it looks like someone from your family brought a bunch of groceries and made a bunch of food," he said, opening the fridge and cabinets. "Here's a note," he said, getting ready to walk it to me.

I waved at him to read it.

Uncle Wylie bought a bunch of groceries for you that will make quick meals as you heal—your mom and aunt refused to allow me to go to the grocery store! So, I stayed home and baked you a pineapple upside down cake, made you some homemade noodles, and made my spaghetti and meatballs with the homemade sauce you love. That should hold you over for a while.

Love,

Grandma

Keith prepared a cup of tea, ice water, and a slice of cake for me, then headed off to take care of the cats.

I took my pills and realized that I had just naturally called Meiser "Mick." I realized I was getting comfortable with him. Then remembered I had contacted Star last night and that she would probably be over today once she got my message. I checked my phone and saw I had a confirming text from her that she might be over around two instead of three. I hadn't had a chance to tell Meiser yet. I looked at my watch and realized he would be back before then. I'd fill him in then.

Keith came back in. "It looks like he took care of everything."

"Grab some cake—it's delicious," I said, forking a huge piece in my mouth.

"No thanks," he said.

"Oh, boy, whatever you have to tell me must be a doozy. I've never known you to turn down this cake before," I said, sitting the cake on the coffee table next to me.

"I wasn't even sure if this is the right time to tell you with everything that just happened. I still don't know if I should tell you now or not," he said, fidgeting with his hands as his eyes diverted back and forth in thought.

"Well, now you *have* to tell me," I said.

"You asked who Mr. Milano was at the town meeting last week—the one who owns M&M's Italian restaurant," he said, gulping my water.

"You know who it is? Is it someone we know?" I was confused by his behavior.

"Yeah, you know him really well," he said as tears filled his eyes.

I shook my head side to side. M&M's—Mick Meiser—Mick Milano? No—couldn't be.

"Okay, who is it?" I really didn't want it confirmed.

"It's Meiser," he said.

I tried to think, but my mind was numb. The pain was gone, but my mind was disoriented—too many thoughts or no thoughts at all. I wasn't sure. I was in shock.

"Go," I said quietly.

"I can't leave you here alone, Jolie."

"Now—get out," I said louder this time.

"Let me call your mom or grandma or Ava—who do you want here with you?" Keith asked.

"I want to be alone—need to be alone—lock doors on your way out," I said in robotic language.

"I don't feel right about—"

I interrupted him, tears streaming down my face and pain in my voice. "Please, Keith, I'm begging you—leave me alone—don't call anyone—I need time to digest this alone—it's light out—I promise to call someone in a few hours to come back here—right now—I need—I—I just—I need." I put my head in my hands and scrunched into the covers on the couch. I turned to face the cushions and pushed my face into the cushion, screaming in emotional pain.

Keith walked up and put his hand on my back. I jerked away. "I said GET OUT—GET OUT—GET OUT—GET OUT!" I screamed. Keith stumbled to the door.

"I'm locking it; I'll leave you alone—I'll call Ava in two hours to have her come here," he said and quickly left.

Oh no, oh no, oh no—how could I do it again— why can't I learn—why do I trust men—why do I trust men? I hate him—hate him—hate him. I hate myself—I'm dumb—worthless—all those things that my biological father made me feel—why didn't I believe him? Because he was right—I am dumb and worthless. Too trusting—how could I, of all people believe in fairy tales?

"Help me, pllleeeeeseeee—help me pleeeeessse— " I begged the universe. "I'm so sorry—what have I done? What have I done?"

I pulled my face out of the cushion as Bobbi Jo jumped on my hip with her little body and began head bumping me on my cheek. "Mommy is sorry, sweetie—I'm okay, I'll be okay," I said.

I turned over and saw my sweet baby moo cow kitty, Lenny Lee, with his large body and long legs and huge puppy paws (even though he is a cat), looking at me in concern. Sammy Jr was cowering in the corner and D.J. was at the foot of my couch. I have never in my life been able to understand how any person could hurt an animal. People have let me down my entire life—but I've always had pets in my life, and they love me at my best and my worst. Why would anyone want to hurt something that gave you unconditional love?

"I'm so sorry, guys—I'm okay—I'll be okay," I said, working to position myself to pet all of them.

I lay back on the couch and let my mind and body rest from my emotional breakdown. Between that and the pain pills and my sweet cats loving on me, I fell back into a deep sleep.

I awoke from Bobbi Jo walking on Lenny, who then yowled on the ground by me.

"Huh?" I said, feeling like I had just had a horrible nightmare.

Then, it all rushed back to me: the attack, the tender way Meiser had cared for me, our exchange of feelings for one another, Keith's words. The tears came back full blown, then I heard the knock at my door.

I couldn't figure out why Ava wouldn't just come in, but then I couldn't remember if I had given her a key to the deadbolts.

I fought the pain to get up and inched slowly to the door to unlock it.

Star stood staring at me. Oh no. I had forgotten

everything—Meiser didn't know she was coming. Okay, all I had to do was play dumb and talk to her about the cross-selling. My body began to tremble all over at the thought that she was the one who violently shoved, kicked, and was ready to bash my face in the curb. I couldn't think—panic swept through my body, and I fought to be normal against the pain, fear, and grogginess of the pain pills.

"Oh no, you poor thing, I'm so sorry you had to get up. We really could have done this another day—you are so brave," Star said, giving me an out.

"You know, Star—you are right. I have no idea what I was thinking last night. I am not able to meet right now, and I meant to call and cancel, but I took a pain pill and fell asleep. Would you hate me if I asked if we could reschedule?" I asked.

"Oh gosh, of course! You look like you can barely walk—let me help you to the couch first, though, and make sure you have everything you need," she said, pushing through the door and taking me in her arms to help me to the couch. She moved swiftly, and pain shot through my stomach, side, and hips.

"Owww..." I moaned as she plopped me indifferently on the couch.

"Sorry, I'm not used to caring for people. Let me get you something to drink before I leave," she said, taking my water glass from the coffee table and moving toward the kitchen. My four cats stayed close to me. I forgot that Meiser—or Milano—had Stewart here. He came walking around the corner toward the cats.

"You really don't need to do that, Star—I'm so tired. Ava should be here any second." I hoped she'd be here—I had no clue when Keith left or when Ava was coming. For that matter, Mick could be coming back.

Star was in the kitchen for what seemed an eternity and came back out with a glass of iced tea. White flakes floated in the tea.

"I thought some iced tea might be nice—I put some sweetener in it since I saw it sitting out," she said, handing it to me.

I sat it down on the table, not daring to take a drink.

"Not thirsty?" she asked. "Don't worry, I didn't put any window cleaner in it like I did poor Mrs. Seevers' drink the other night."

I shook my head, afraid if I spoke, she'd hear the tremble in my voice. I forced out, "Why would you want to hurt her?"

"I was so sick of listening to her talk about the prices on the menu. She kept comparing the food to yours. She told me she had some leftover cornbread from your restaurant that day and she'd bring some in for me to try. I figured I'd give her a little dose of window cleaner, then put it in her ear that it very well could be from your food. She said her husband doesn't like spicy food, so she had a lot left."

"You hate me that much?"

"Nah, I don't hate you. Come on; you need to eat and drink to keep your strength up, Jolie," she said, walking toward the tea and picking it up. She was looming over me.

I felt like I had stopped breathing completely. I wished I could think straight. Stewart jumped up on my lap, blocking Star from me.

She leaned forward and pushed him off me.

"Here, let me help you take a drink," she said,

leaning down and grabbing my chin with her one hand roughly. "Someone must have kicked you hard for you to be so out of it," she said, slamming a hand into my side.

"Nooooo!" I yelled out as she took that opportunity to pour tea down my throat. I tried to spit it out, but she grabbed my nose and held it and pushed my chin up—some tea spilled out of my mouth, and I swallowed some.

"I used to live in a nice safe world like you—I used to be a decent person like you. I thought Mick and I would make a great couple, get married, have kids someday. Then, my mom had her stroke. Jared—her financial advisor, took off with her money. Olive and I couldn't afford to put her in a nice home and my whole life changed in one minute when some incompetent idiot gave her the wrong medication that killed her."

"I'm so sorry, Star," I said through terrified sobs.

"Are you sorry? I'll bet you're sorry—what are you? Twenty-two, twenty-three? I'm sure you know what pain is with your long curly locks, pretty and sweet blue eyes, and that Barbie-doll face. Sure, you know pain, don't you?" She punched me in the ribs again as I gasped for air.

"I know pain," I gasped.

"Only the pain I make you feel," she said with a crazed look in her eyes.

"Not—true," I said between sharp breaths of agony.

"Oh yeah, little one, what's your pain, girlfriend? Do share!" She sat next to me, and I saw she was holding one my butcher knives.

"Star, my biological father was abusive in many ways. My stepdad was like my real father. He died of cancer several years back—he got me and stayed in my life in spite of not being blood-related—" I tried to get as much truth out as possible for her to see I was human.

She interrupted me with a fake caring expression. "Daddy issues? That figures—no wonder Mick wants to save you," she spat out.

I heard a loud knock at the door and went to scream. Star pounced on me and put her hand over my mouth, the knife to my throat. "One noise and I'll slit your throat, princess."

I believed her.

I heard Meiser yelling from outside. "Jolie, are you in there? Keith found me and lit into me. I know you know everything. I'm so sorry. I can explain," he yelled. "Please let me explain!"

Tears raced down my cheeks as Star whispered, "Isn't that sweet? So, you found out he isn't who he said he is, huh? I tried to warn you." She giggled hysterically into my ear. "You know he was there for me when my mom died—we grew up together. I can tell you so much about him and his family—but I guess you will never know," she said, digging the point of the knife into my throat. I felt blood dribble down my neck.

I'd never been so terrified in my life.

Meiser continued calling me from outside.

"You know that he met you not too long after my mom died," Star said. "I still needed him, but he decided to move to this stupid little village to be near you—you little tramp! My friend, Nestle—he always had a thing for me—I used it to get back at you," she continued, giggling manically. "I have a way with men—talking Meiser into building his restaurant in case he couldn't be a detective from the MS, telling him how much it could help me, Olive, Gaze, and him. I thought it could help reunite us—but there you were. Then I heard about Lou— just like Jared swindling people out of money. I did hire Mrs. Seevers—least I could do. See, I'm not all bad." She rubbed the blade of the knife up and down my cheek. "I so wanted to bash this pretty face into the curb."

Meiser had moved to the window and must have seen the scene. "STAR! NO!!!!" he yelled.

This frightened the cats and Lenny moved right under Star's feet as Bobbi lunged at her with those claws Ava was so frightened of. When Star jumped back, she fell over Lenny, and I screamed bloody murder. The adrenaline rushed through my body. I jumped over the couch as pain pierced my body and limped as quickly to the door as I could. Star pushed her way up and jumped at me, catching my robe and pulling. I let the robe pull off me and fell into the door, unlocking it.

Star raced toward me with the knife lifted as Meiser opened the door and fired his gun at her in midleap. She fell to the ground.

Chapter Eighteen

Several days had passed since the incident, as I chose to call it for now. I had been hospitalized and treated for poison and now broken ribs—with a lot more bruises and cuts.

Ava told me she and my family had cleaned up my house and had someone out to put new carpet in from the blood on the floor. The first thing she did when I came to was to reassure me all of my cats were okay.

I hadn't wanted to talk to anyone very much. Meiser—or Milano—wanted to see me, but no one in my family was allowing that to happen, even if he had saved my life.

Chief Tobias came to visit me now that I was able to be more aware of my surroundings.

"I'm sorry I couldn't figure all of this out before she got to you," Teddy said, unable to make eye contact.

"It's not your fault that she snapped—I'm not even sure it's her fault," I said.

Teddy looked at me. "How can you feel any sympathy for her?"

"I've been hurt too. Everyone reacts to things differently. Things piled up on her—she felt out of control, and things spiraled out of control." I shrugged my shoulders. "After everything that's happened this past year, I'm going to have to give some thought to therapy."

"No wonder Mesier is in love with you," he said, then bit his lip. "Shoot, I'm sorry."

"That's not his name," I said.

"I know. I didn't know—I swear," he said.

"Do you know why he did it?" I wanted someone unbiased to explain it all to me. I knew if I listened to Ava, Keith, or anyone in my family, I wouldn't get the entire truth—not that they would mean to be biased. But they would be.

"I only know so much. There is something about his past with his father—he had his name legally changed a long time ago. He wasn't trying to fool anyone with that. I'm not making excuses for him—just telling you what I know to be true," he said, looking concerned that I would be angered.

"That's why I'm asking you, Teddy. I want the truth—not a version where someone is sugarcoating it or trying to sway my emotions," I said.

"I don't know the entire story about his past—I don't think he wants people to know," he said. "I did find out about the MS. We found out that Nestle was the one who purchased all the land around the Italian restaurant."

"That doesn't surprise me," I said.

"Well, this guy has his hand in a lot of shady business, including how he bought the land. Our legal team is on it, and I've got him held in a cell for interfering in an ongoing investigation. He knew what Star did, and we believe he may have been a part of coercing her into doing it," Teddy said.

"She seemed vulnerable—I felt like her laugh was manic. Is she okay?" I asked.

Teddy shook his head slowly. "Star was seriously wounded. She is alive, but in a coma right now."

Wow, that was odd after what had happened to her mom.

"Nestle is connected to Mayor Cardinal in some way, but no one can seem to finger Cardinal for anything," he said, shaking his head again.

"I don't trust that guy," I said.

"Nestle is probably his fall guy—he doesn't seem at all concerned that he's being held," Teddy said.

"I think we need to sit down and have another village meeting with Mayor Nalini," I said.

"Maybe more of a private meeting if you want to get at the truth. I've heard our mayor got in on Lou's—which turned out to be Nestle's financial scheme—possibly Cardinal's scheme—it's going to take some time to sort through it all. Good news is that, for now, the village property is safe, and the property sale is stalled until further investigation," Teddy said. "Anyway, nothing for you to think about right now. You need to focus on resting and healing."

"True," I said. I would have to speak to Meiser— Milano—at some point, though.

Epilogue

Star remained in a coma for the next several months before she died. Olive was devastated at the loss of her sister, and moved back to Tri-City with Gaze. I couldn't blame Olive for wanting to get out of Leavensport after everything that happened.

Delilah stood strong and never sold her building, nor did her parents.

Nestle had some high-powered attorney working for him. I was so busy healing that I didn't even know he was let out of jail within a week of being put in. As Mayor Nalini kept saying, urban sprawl is not illegal, and they couldn't pin anything on Nestle or Mayor Cardinal. It made me wonder more about Mick's brother, who had been mayor, and if he was involved in any of this business.

Speaking of Mick, he continued to try and worm his way back into my life. Between Ava and my family, they kept him at bay while I continued to heal physically. Eventually, we ran into each other. It was inevitable in our small village.

We had a brief conversation outside of the library one rainy afternoon late summer. He apologized and wanted to meet for a long conversation. I told him I thought that was a good idea. Yet, I still needed time—and I told him so. Mentally, I still had a lot of work to do. I realized much had been weighing on me from the events of the past year. Also, I had to admit that I'd never healed from things that happened to me as a child. He understood. He wasn't happy about it, but he agreed to give me space and I told him I would call him once I had time to figure some things out.

Mayor Nalini had stated at the town meeting many months ago that he planned to invest more in the safety of the community. Zed Zimmerman told me at the restaurant one day that he heard urban sprawl causes an increase in crime. His theory was that was why Mayor Nalini wanted to do more to keep our town safe. I had no idea if that was true or not.

The mayor did hire a forensic therapist to work at the station. Tabitha Turner would soon be opening an office on the west side of town. I had already asked Teddy to give her my name and information to call me when I could schedule an appointment.

The rise and fall of my love life were finally evening out. I didn't plan on moving forward with anything until I understood myself better.

Recipe for Jalapeño Cheddar Cornbread

Ingredients

2 jalapeño peppers, seeds* removed and diced

1 1/4 cups all-purpose flour

1 cup fine cornmeal

1 tbsp baking powder

1 1/2 tsp kosher salt (1 tsp. if using fine salt)

4 large eggs

1 cup cooked corn kernels plus enough cream, milk, or buttermilk** to equal 1 1/2 cups

1 cup grated cheddar cheese*** plus bit more for top before baking

3/4 cup unsalted butter at room temperature

2/3 cup sugar

*see Notes

Instruct ions

Place diced jalapeños in skillet, then place in a 10-inch top diameter cast iron skillet in cold oven on middle rack. Preheat oven to 400°F and leave skillet with jalapeños in oven as it preheats. Check periodically to make sure they aren't burning and to give them a quick stir. Remove when they are lightly browned and allow to cool. Return skillet immediately to oven.

In a small bowl, whisk together the flour, cornmeal, baking powder, and salt. Set aside.

In a medium bowl, lightly beat eggs. Whisk in corn/cream mixture and cheddar cheese. Set aside.

In a large bowl, mix butter and sugar with a wooden spoon,**** just until butter absorbs the sugar. Add the egg mixture and mix until just combined. Stir in the cooled jalapeños. Mix in the dry ingredients just until barely incorporated.

Remove skillet from oven and lightly coat with nonstick spray. Spoon batter into hot pan and quickly top with a bit more grated cheddar cheese. Bake cornbread until top is golden brown and springs back when gently pressed, 25-28 minutes when baked in a 10-inch skillet (may be longer if your skillet is smaller). Let cool 10 minutes before serving.

Recipe Notes

*If you like your food extra spicy, then leave the seeds in the jalapeños.

**This means you add the corn kernels to a measuring cup first, then pour in the milk until the milk rises to the 1 1/2 cup level. (I was not able to find buttermilk at my local store. If you have the same problem, then you can add one tablespoon of lemon juice or vinegar for every one cup of milk.)

***I'm a cheese lover—I added an extra half cup of cheese!

****I tried the recipe mixing with a wooden spoon and again using my Kitchenette mixer. Call me crazy, but I truly believe it tasted better when using the wooden spoon to stir ingredients.

This recipe was adapted from seasonsandsuppas.ca and foodiecrush.com.

Recipe for Dutch Cast Iron Pork Loin*

Ingredients

4 -5 lbs pork roast (butt, loin, etc.)

1 tbsp lard

5 garlic cloves, peeled

1 small onion, thinly sliced

2 cups water

1 tbsp Kitchen Bouquet

2 tsp black pepper

1 tsp salt

2 tbsp cornstarch

1/2 cup water

Instructions

Preheat oven to 350°F.

Melt lard in cast iron Dutch oven over medium high heat.

Salt and pepper all sides of pork roast.

When lard just begins to give off smell of being hot, place roast in pot.

DO NOT move it for a minute or so, then rotate it to brown all sides.

Lay garlic cloves and onion slices around the roast and stir to brown them a bit.

Mix Kitchen Bouquet into the 2 cups of water.

Pour in the water mixture.

Bring to a boil.

Cover tightly and place in lower portion of the oven.

Roast 1 hour for boneless roast; 1 3/4 hours for bone-in roast.

Halfway through roasting time, turn the roast over.

Remove roast from pan and cover to keep hot.

Mix 2 tbsp cornstarch into 1/2 cup water.

Using a whisk, stir the cornstarch mixture into the pot drippings, breaking up the garlic cloves as you mix.

Bring to a boil, taste and season if needed with salt and/or pepper.

*This recipe was adapted from geniuskitchen.com.

Recipe for Cast Iron Chicken Marsala

Ingredients

1/4 cup unsalted butter

1 (8-ounce) package fresh baby portobello mushrooms, quartered

2 shallots, thinly sliced

2 tbsp olive oil

6 (4 ounce) chicken cutlets

1 tsp kosher salt

1 tsp ground black pepper

1/4 cup all-purpose flour

1/2 cup chicken broth

1/3 cup Marsala wine

1 tbsp chopped fresh thyme

1/4 cup heavy whipping cream

Garnish: fresh thyme

Instructions

In a 12-inch cast iron skillet, melt butter over medium-high heat. Add mushrooms and shallots; cook until tender, 3 to 4 minutes. Remove from skillet.

Add oil to skillet. Sprinkle chicken with salt and pepper. Place flour in a small dish. Dredge chicken in flour, shaking off excess. Add chicken to skillet; cook until browned, about 4 minutes per side.

Remove from skillet.

Add broth, wine, and thyme to skillet; cook, stirring constantly, until mixture begins to thicken. Stir in cream. Return mushrooms, shallot, and chicken to skillet, turning chicken to coat. Garnish with thyme, if desired, Serve immediately.

Book Three Turkey Basted to Death Coming November 15, 2019

Jolie Tucker's life is about to change. Her best friend Ava's family is back for the Thanksgiving holiday from Santa Domingo. The wacky duo is hard at work setting up a Leavensport village holiday gathering at Village Community Center. The holiday takes a turn when families from the inner city unexpectedly show up, and the women have to think quick on their feet to find enough food to feed everyone.. Jolie is doing her best to keep her emotions in check after starting therapy after the incident with Meiser last summer. Things get worse quickly when the Tri-City teen advocate leader is found face down in the turkey with a baster sticking out of her ear.

Chapter one of Turkey Basted to Death

The times are for sure a-changing. This time last year I actually thought I was ready to *maybe* try dating again. My life ran the course of that topsy-turvy thing called love—and I feel like I fell off, flat on my face, when the ride was at the top of the hill. That's where I am now. Eating pavement.

"Aren't you supposed to be picking up your family at the airport now?" I asked Ava.

"They aren't getting in until later tonight. Papa wanted to finish up some last-minute work so he could enjoy the holiday," Ava said, while testing out the fifth turkey recipe I had tried that week.

It's Thanksgiving this Thursday and with Ava's family coming back to Leavensport, we decided to rent out the community center. The majority of the village is sharing Thanksgiving together. All of the restaurants in town are contributing to the dinner and many of the villagers are making lots of food, like a potluck. I'd been testing out multiple recipes for the turkeys for the day. We were doing taste tests at the restaurant so the villagers could choose their favorites, and sharing the remainder of the turkeys with the homeless shelter in Tri-City. So far, the Cajun turkey was a big hit, as well as the smokehouse turkey and honey turkey with lemon and sage.

"Is your therapist going to be at the Thanksgiving gathering?" Ava asked.

"I don't know. Why would you ask that?" I

asked.

"Isn't that a conflict of interest? The two of you can't have dinner together, can you?"

"She is my counselor, not my parole officer."

"Yeah, I know that. I'm just asking if it's a conflict of interest. Geesh!"

"You and my family know I'm seeing her. It's not a secret, but I'm not posting it on social media or anything. Everything I say is confidential. It's not like she will sit at the table and share everything I've told her."

Ava's glare made me take notice that my hands were on my hips. I must have been giving her a look, not to mention I had used the "duh" tone with her. She was not happy with me at the moment.

"You know what, forget it! I hope she does you some good. Your moods have been all over the place lately," Ava harrumphed.

Flinching, I reached out and lightly touched her arm. "I'm sorry. I know I'm all over the place lately. Honestly, I don't know if she will be there or not. If she is, I doubt I will talk to her much. She's nice enough, but we're not friends. Also, it is awkward living in a small village and seeing her all over the place. Truthfully, it seems we both avoid each other when out in public. Which seems weird sometimes."

"I can understand that."

"Are you excited to see your family finally?" I changed the topic.

"I'm nervous. We've never been away from each other for this long. What if they've changed a lot or if I've changed a lot? My mom is still doing that manipulative dance with me, being passive-aggressive about me deciding not to move with them," Ava said.

"Don't worry, they will be thrilled to see you!"

Our cook, Carlos, popped his head into the kitchen. "Ah, Miss Jolie, you will want to come to front."

Ava followed me out. "Hello, Mayor Nalini, how can we help you?"

"Hi, ladies, any thoughts about the Thanksgiving gathering?" he asked.

Ava and I raised our eyebrows at each other quizzically. "Nope, just been testing out different recipes for turkeys. We've been working on the menu and taste tests the last week."

"Okay, that's great. And, Ava, excited to see your family?" the mayor asked.

"Sure, it will be good to see them again." She fumbled with her hands.

"Is there a problem?" I asked.

"What? Problem? No—of course not." The mayor shifted. "Actually, Ava, wouldn't you rather have a nice private dinner, seeing that you and your family haven't had time together for a while?"

"No," Ava drug out the word. "They can't stay long and this will make things easy on them to get to visit with everyone at one time. We will have time to visit before they leave."

"What is going on, Mayor?" I asked.

"I just got off the phone with Mayor Cardinal in Tri-City," he began.

Oh no, I felt my heart sink into my chest. Whatever he was about to say could not be good news.

About the Author

Moving into her second decade working in education, Jodi Rath has decided to begin a life of crime in her The Cast Iron Skillet Mystery Series. Her passion for both mysteries and education led her to combine the two to create her business MYS ED, where she splits her time between working as an adjunct for Ohio teachers and creating mischief in her fictional writing. She currently resides in a small, cozy village in Ohio with her husband and her nine cats.

Links so we can Stay Connected

Be sure to sign up for a monthly newsletter to get MORE of the Leavensport gang with free flash fiction, short stories, two-minute mysteries, cast iron recipes, tips and more. Subscribe to our monthly newsletter for a FREE Mystery A Month at http://eepurl.com/dIfXdb

Follow me on Facebook at https://www.facebook.com/authorjodirath

@jodirath is where you can find me on Twitter

Upcoming Release Dates

Coming November 15

Seasonal Book 2.5 in **The Cast Iron Skillet Mystery Series** *Turkey Basted to Death*

Coming February 28, 2020

Book Three in **The Cast Iron Skillet Mystery Series** *Blueberry Cobbler Blackmail*

CPSIA information can be obtained
at www.ICGtesting.com
Printed in the USA
LVHW030100140121
676401LV00014B/1523

9 780578 537825